I0679024

Hurt To Healing
The Book

LaTrice Williams

Copyright © 2014 LaTrice Williams

First Edition.

Publisher: Bridges & Channels Enterprises, LLC.

Cover Design: A. Deese of Bountifully Blessed Publishing Services.

Cover Art: Corbis (#42-23055860).

All rights reserved. No part of this publication may be reproduced, stored in a retrieval system or transmitted in any form or by any means without the prior written consent of the Author and Publisher. Exceptions are brief quotations within critical articles and reviews.

This work of fiction is loosely based on a true story. Names, places, and some events have been changed to protect the innocent and the privacy of those even remotely connected to the story. All song lyrics and titles have been properly cited within the text.

Scriptures were taken from the HOLY BIBLE: King James Version, New International Version and the Message Bible.

ISBN: 0991234014
ISBN-13: 978-0-9912340-1-1

DEDICATED TO HEALING PEOPLE

Hurting people are healing people regardless of how long the process takes you.

AUTHOR'S CONTACT INFO

Email:
LaTriceSpeaks@latricewilliams.com

Main Website:
www.latricewilliams.com

Facebook:
www.facebook.com/LaTriceWilliamsMinistries

Twitter:
https://www.twitter.com/LaTriceSpeaks

ACKNOWLEDGMENTS & SPECIAL THANKS:

To My Lord and Savior, Jesus Christ – Your life saved my life. For loving me through my good and my bad: Thank You. All of my life, I'll serve You. Thank You for not erasing my future because of my past. I give You my highest praise – Hallelujah! There are no other words to express my thanks and love!

In Loving Memory of Mother Eula Mae Haynes – Momma, love is the word that describes you best. You showed love to me and so many others. I honor God for your life because your life changed mine.

To my children, the apple of my eye – Always remember to keep God first in all you do. All my love to you.

Bridges & Channels Enterprises – WOW! What a great learning experience! God bless you for your guidance, your belief in my work and the countless hours you've put into making this writing what it should be. You have helped me to ensure that the message was clearly revealed to those who need it the most. You are one of a kind! Thank you for caring, sharing and teaching your authors one work at a time!

CHAPTER ONE
Meet Maiya and Nicole

During the drive to her home, Chamaiya LaShelle Jackson aka 'Maiya' was quiet as usual after speaking or preaching. Though she'd shed plenty of tears earlier today during yet another liberating message, they started rolling again as flashbacks of just where she'd actually come from flooded her soul.

Her assistant, Angela Fortson aka 'Angie', looked over at her and nodded in understanding. She was closer to Maiya than most and so was used to this routine by now. Thus there would be no interruptions during this time of quiet reflection, those precious moments of just resting in God's presence.

As Maiya reflected upon her life, her mind seemed to always end up back at Nicole's house. Nicole, her biological mother, who didn't seem like a mother and certainly didn't act like a mother. Today her thoughts revisited what her life was like during her teen years, many of which were spent under Nicole's roof.

* * * * *

At fourteen, Maiya was once again crying her eyes out. Just when she felt like she could finally live her life, Nicole dropped yet another bomb on her. This one was like never before.

This time Maiya had to take care of Destiny, Lil' Joe and Damon – her younger siblings. That was foolery at its best. Why? Because it was either Nicole's children or her boyfriends and everyone knows who she chose again. Same as usual.

Why? Why? Why? Maiya thought as she sat in her room, fuming over the phone call she just had with her mother. Inside, she was raging mad and hurting terribly. *I didn't have those kids. They're not mine.*

Don't get it wrong, Maiya loved her siblings. But she was excited and looking forward to enjoying this time in her life, not being somebody's surrogate mother. Nicole *would* pull this crap when she was getting ready to go to high school.

Maiya really shouldn't have been too surprised. It was just like her mother to do something like this. Of course Nicole masked her real reason for throwing that bomb, claiming that she had to work and be away so much with her job. Yet experience told Maiya that it was about a man. That's a check the bank would definitely cash. The *way* Nicole dropped that bomb confirmed that fact.

"Maiya, you are moving back here and taking care of these kids. I have work and other stuff and I don't have time for you and your mess! I don't really care how you feel or what you're about to do. You're coming BACK!" Nicole had yelled harshly into the phone.

"Yeah, other stuff I bet," Maiya replied with much attitude. "Nicole, I don't know why you are doing this to me. You don't even want me and I'm not their mother. I'm their sister!" She clenched the phone tightly. If she held it any tighter, she would break it.

Nicole screamed out her response. "Didn't I just say I don't care? You're the reason my life is so hard now. You're coming over here if I have to drag you, do you hear me?"

Each time Nicole said, '*I don't care*', Maiya felt utterly assaulted. It was an internal wound that continued to build with each verbal assault inflicted upon her. Her rage and anger continued to build as well. She'd been aware of those too. She just hadn't known what to do about them. Yet she quickly figured out how to stop the verbal abuse.

Click!

That's right. Maiya hung up the phone in Nicole's face. It was the first time, but certainly not the last. This quickly became a pattern for her. If you started talking crazy, then you could just start talking to the operator.

The 'click' happened mostly with Nicole. Maiya just couldn't take her sometimes. Every conversation was, '*it's your fault this*' and '*it's your fault that*'. She was just plain sick of it *and* her.

Was it disrespectful? Yes, but the truth was she had absolutely NO respect; not one drop or ounce, for this woman.

And who could forget about all the men Nicole had? She had more men than the law allowed. She was engaged more times than even she could count. It was like she was on an '*I'm getting married no matter who he is*' kick, especially after dealing with a married man and not being able to have him. That experience did something to Nicole and ultimately to Maiya as well.

In fact, everything that happened to her mother left lasting impressions upon Maiya. Some good. Some not so good. She didn't know it then, but generational curses were being sown in her young life. Curses on top of curses.

That's partly why Nicole got the 'click' even though it wasn't right. It was why Maiya made up her mind not to listen to her crap anymore and why she didn't respect Nicole even though she was her mother.

If only she was like Momma, Maiya thought, referring to her grandmother whom she wished was her real mother.

Her grandmother was the sweetest, strongest lady she'd ever met and she loved everybody. Momma was the one person Maiya knew loved her.

Before her teenage mind could rest in happier thoughts, the phone rang again. Convinced that it was Nicole calling to continue her relentless tirade of foolishness, Maiya politely picked the phone up and slammed it down.

Leaving the house soon thereafter, she headed to her part-time job at Wendy's, not thinking anything more about that encounter with Nicole. As far as she was concerned, the matter was over. Done. Solved and Re-solved. She was not going back to that house and that was that.

At least she thought it was...

Nicole showed up three days later to *make* her go back to her house. Imagine that, Maiya was living with another family by this time, yet she still couldn't escape her mother's torment or the responsibility of Nicole's children. That was a hot mess if she'd ever seen one.

* * * * *

Maiya briefly tensed up in her seat as her teenage concerns came echoing from the past, dragging old feelings of sadness with them. Her deepest concerns at the time had been – *What about all the things I want for my life? How will I ever get there?*

Maiya didn't know where 'there' was back then, but she was sure Nicole's house wasn't it. She had so many hopes and dreams that seemed to be fading with each day of raising three children that she didn't have. She didn't blame them, but at times she felt like that whole situation was holding her back in many ways or at least had the potential to do so.

Maiya suddenly smiled. *God knew where 'there' was. He brought me to my place of purpose,* she thought, relaxing in her seat again as her ride down memory lane continued.

CHAPTER TWO
A Few Silver Linings

Going deeper into her reflections, Maiya recalled how attending church was one thing that seemed to help relieve some of her teenage burdens. The only thing she liked and disliked equally was that people had no real idea what was going on in her life at the time or so she thought. She liked it because she didn't have to worry about discussing or having to explain the absence of her mother. She disliked it because as much as she liked church, nobody understood that this was a 'break' for her.

Truth be told, Sunday was like a party for Maiya and her siblings. Don't get it twisted, they learned that Bible. Pastor didn't play. But there were times that all they did was sit in the back of the church and talk through the whole sermon, passing notes. They even had the nerve to shout before the music could get started good. Some people don't know anything about that, but it happens.

Another blessing to Maiya was Mama Ludie. Ludie Star was the mother of her best friend, Elise, who she'd gone to stay with briefly. Mama Ludie always helped out, called, and checked to make sure she was okay. She became her 'mama' in so many ways.

Although Mama Ludie didn't have Maiya biologically, she sure treated her like her own child. At least that's how it felt. She missed out on that type of mothering at Nicole's house. The fact of the matter is, she missed out on a lot of stuff being at that house of torment.

At the time, Maiya didn't know how to tell Mama Ludie what she was *really* feeling and doing, and not have alarms sounded. How in the world could she reveal that she was paying bills like a grown woman at home, sometimes not eating so everyone else could and actively playing somebody's mother as if she actually had a clue how to fill that role? A mess.

Life eventually taught her how to be a mother or rather it seemed that way. If nothing else, it certainly taught her what kind of mother *not* to be.

Maiya's first example of how *not* to be a mother came when Nicole basically abandoned her as a child, leaving her in the care of her grandmother for many years. Although Maiya rarely spoke of that time in her life, it was something that never left her mind or her heart. Granted, being left with Momma turned out to be the best thing for her, but it still had a lasting effect on her.

As much as Maiya wanted to tell it all at times, she knew it would only make matters worse. Nicole had everybody convinced that she was only there to 'help out' while she worked. Besides, there were enough red flags as it were.

Had Maiya told Mama Ludie, she could just see her cutting the darn fool on Nicole. Mama Ludie was a quiet lady, but she could go there if need be. That really would have been a sight to see.

Then there was Dad – the title Maiya gave her uncle Charlie, who helped out and tried to make sure she and her siblings had what they needed when he could. Well, at least he did when she would finally call and ask for some help. Maiya could be stubborn to the utmost sometimes.

Besides Daddy Ollie, who was Mama Ludie's husband, Charlie was the next thing to a daddy considering she'd never met her biological father. That's a whole 'nother soap opera in itself.

Right now Maiya concentrated on how God had a purpose and plan for her life even back then. How in the midst of her teenage torments He gave her a daily escape – school. Northside High School – School of Performing Arts to be exact.

Maiya sighed and smiled, remembering third and fourth period class – the real reason she absolutely loved school so much. Within that time slot was…wait for it…CHORUS!

Being in Mrs. Dee Merit's class was the best thing that could have happened to her at school. As lead alto, Maiya was held in high regards by her music teacher as well as her peers, girls and guys alike. She was highly esteemed by one peer in particular – Tony Blackwell.

At 6'3, Tony had dark chocolate skin, dark brown eyes, and soft wavy black hair. Built like a football player, he was two hundred and sixty pounds of pure hunk.

Although the little crew that Maiya hung with and sometimes sang with thought Tony was gorgeous, too, none of them dared to like him romantically. Everyone knew that she had Tony's heart. She'd captured it without even trying to.

Maiya continued to hold Tony's heart for many years to come, even now. He adored her and for some reason, nothing or no one could change that.

How did Maiya feel about Tony back then? Well, let's just say that he was her favorite friend although she failed to tell him that for many years.

Maiya recalled how Tony would approach her every day as the class finished rehearsing the first hour, just after the bell rang for the first break. He would do so before she could even get out of her seat. His greeting was always the same and always positive.

"Hey beautiful," Tony would say in a genuine tone.

"Hey, Tony! You're so crazy, boy. You say that every day." Maiya would blush, despite her attempt to dismiss his compliment. She liked it even if she wouldn't admit it. It wasn't something she heard often or actually from any other source.

"What is so crazy about me calling you beautiful? You are."

"Okay, okay. If you say so." She wanted and needed to accept his words as true even if she didn't show it or believe it within herself most times.

"How are you? You look tired." As usual, he was always so perceptive.

"I am a little tired, but I'm fine." Maiya *was* tired that day, but she was a socialite to her heart and could hang with the best of them. Tired or not, she kept going.

Over the years, she introverted and that socialite disappeared. Life...life has a way of changing a person from the inside out.

As Maiya stood in the hallway continuing her conversation with Tony that day, she spoke to more of her friends while they waited for the second part of class to start. Half listening to the conversations going on around her, she saw a very interesting someone enter their classroom. A cute male someone with a bad boy vibe. Mr. Interesting's name was Jeron.

Ding, ding, ding!

Though Maiya kept her face neutral, her sneaky mind quickly went to work on how to add him to her collection of boyfriends. She had to have him and she *would* have him...until she was done with him. Life had turned her into a dog-eat-dog Maiya and sadly she was good at it. Almost as good as she was at cursing. A hot mess!

As the bell rang to start the second hour of chorus, she and Tony returned to the classroom. As usual, he pecked her on the cheek and returned to his seat. She just shook her head, unwilling to even think about venturing out of the friendship zone with him.

Although Tony was sweet, Maiya was too partial to bad boys to give him that kind of consideration. She was also too vain and entirely too hot in the tail back then. Plus she really didn't want to hurt such a nice guy. A guy that showed her how a young lady *should* be treated.

In later years, Maiya would have loved that type of genuine affection in her life. But at that time, her mind was somewhere else. Believe that! Besides, perfect gentleman didn't do too well with fast women.

Maiya winced at the memory of just how fast she was back then. At how much she used to get around. The older she got, the more physically developed she became. The more developed she became, the more men she got. Well, boys anyway.

Interestingly enough, Maiya never did get Tony. Rather she never allowed him to get her. Not back then.

CHAPTER THREE
Look Where He Brought Me To

Praise God! I'm not fast like that now! Maiya thought, grateful that she learned to be fast...or rather quick in other ways. Quick to obey the Lord. Quick to help others in need.

Earlier today God used her to help a packed auditorium of teenagers. Teenagers, who found themselves in awkward and painful situations, standing against criminal allegations, and holding in some very painful secrets. They thought they were alone. They weren't.

Today Maiya made sure they knew just how un-alone they were when she shared her story and experiences with them. She'd done her best to instill some hope into those innocent lives.

Innocent lives?

Yes.

Every bad thing those teenagers had done and every bad place they'd been, had not been on their own nor had it been all their fault. Others had shaped them, directed them, led and misled them. Many people had hurt them.

Yes, those young people had seen and done some regrettable things in their lives, but today they'd been given a chance to start over. Start over spiritually as well as naturally. It was their chance to move on to better things, better places and encounter some much better people.

Today Maiya had offered them a place that didn't necessarily have to hurt. A place where decisions could be made rationally and with clear minds. A place where they could be in control of their God-given destinies.

As Maiya looked out over the crowd of young people, the words seemed to flow from her like water from a faucet. This had not been a mere scheduled event on her calendar. Nor was it a simple chit-chat with the guys and girls. It was a day preordained by God to affect lives, change minds and set someone's path in the right direction.

"A lifetime of hurt has a way of shaping people into someone they never knew they were, someone others don't understand, and oftentimes someone who is yet to understand themselves," had been the first words out of Maiya's mouth today. "They don't understand who they really are, what they really want, how they could possibly obtain it, who they could really be, or who could really love them. Least of all, they don't realize that they can love themselves. They certainly have no real idea that above all, God loves them."

As Maiya spoke, she realized even more how far God had brought her. It was one thing to know it within herself, but to speak it now and know that it had manifested in her life was awe-striking to her.

Smiling, she cleared her throat and continued. "Yes, I'm saying to you that God loves you despite what people say about you, despite the things you may have done. God loves you because He does. This state of blindfolded living and way of negative thinking often remains in our lives until healing takes place."

Maiya went on to explain how blindfolded living was that period in life when people didn't have a clue who they were, who they could be, or that they could be loved. Many people experienced it but didn't quite know how to express it. For her, it was that period of time before she could see clearly concerning herself and the things that she endured.

"Now what kind of healing was I referring to earlier? Divine healing from God!" Maiya continued excitedly. "Healing that causes one to live in peace that surpasses all understanding and guards our hearts and minds. Healing that allows one to experience an inner joy that shows up in the most needed moments. Healing that is not dependent upon what you can do, but what the Master can do *for* you and *through* you. He is able to do all things but fail."

Then Maiya told them how to get that healing and keep it – by faith.

"The Word of God says that we must have faith because without faith it is impossible to please Him. The Bible declares that faith comes by hearing and hearing by the Word of God. Today you are hearing a true Word from God and I sincerely pray that you will embark upon this journey with faith in God, an open mind and a receiving heart. The journey from hurt to healing is not often chosen by most people, but usually comes through living life, loving God, and allowing Him to love you. Young men and women, if you will allow me to speak personally to you today, there is a word from the Lord."

Loud claps and thunderous applause filled the atmosphere. There were smiles and awestruck looks all over the room. That overwhelmingly positive response diminished any nervousness Maiya had. Though she'd been privileged to speak to adult crowds, she wasn't quite sure how she'd be received by a youth audience. To find them so welcoming and accepting had been a true blessing.

Maiya didn't know if they were so welcoming because many had already heard of her or wanted to hear her story for themselves. Maybe they were awestruck because someone with similar experiences had made it out alive and well. Either way she'd been encouraged. Still was.

Today Maiya didn't just give them the opportunity to meet her, hear her story, a one-day speech or a Sunday sermon. No, she offered them the One that sent the message – Jesus Christ, a life-changing, thought-provoking, Spirit-filled, heart-transplanting Savior.

"Thank you, thank you," Maiya said after the applause died down. "It is indeed an honor to be here with you today. To the wonderful administrators of this program and the many people who work so hard to keep it in the top rankings in America, I must say thank you for allowing me this blessed opportunity to stand before these young people and encourage them today. I sincerely hope it will not be my last time. Most of all, I give honor and praise to my Savior, Jesus Christ, who has brought me out of darkness and into a light I would have never known without Him. Without Him, there would be no you or me."

Glancing over the auditorium, she then addressed those that were her main reason for being there. "To you, young men and women, I honor you as well. Your lives deserve to be honored and celebrated, because you have endured some of life's hardest trials and overcome many obstacles. Looking at your faces, it reminds me of the life I endured, the challenges I faced and the victory I've been offered through Jesus Christ. Today God has sent you a message to uplift and encourage you. It is not a coincidence for anyone in this room. So for those who are wondering why you are here in this place, at this time, please know that it is divinely orchestrated regardless of how you got here. Today *this* is where you are *supposed* to be."

People nodded in agreement all across the room. On the right side of the stage was Elise Star, aka 'Star' – the founder of the program and Maiya's childhood best friend.

Star had been a true sister to her even when she wasn't capable of being one in return. She had looked so proud of Maiya today...so proud of the woman that she became. No doubt Mama Ludie was going to hear all about today's event from that particular daughter.

"It is my understanding that many of you have heard of me and my story. You have seen a glimpse into my life. But I'd like to share with you some intimate details and give you a foretaste of what your future can hold. There used to be a time when I told my story, I'd feel defeated all over again. I would clam up and not talk about it. That was until I read the scripture in Revelation 12:11a, which says they were saved by the Blood of the Lamb and the Word of their testimony. This is truly my testimony and I certainly believe that with God at work in me, someone can be saved. In fact, *you* can be saved from your sins and from your fears. I believe that although the story is painful and the memories sometimes are even more painful, the healing that you can receive in the name of Jesus outweighs it all. This opportunity to share my story yet again makes it all worth it. It was not in vain and neither were your experiences."

Maiya acknowledged the fact that she understood that many bad things had happened to them. Hurt, neglect, and abandonment. She was familiar with all of those and more. She also addressed the fact that some of them had done bad things to others. She knew about that life too.

"You're not alone, first and foremost, because God loves you and has promised to never leave you nor forsake you. We have the promise that God will be with us even until the end of the earth. Secondly, you're not alone, because it's apparent that the people in this facility have put in long hours, sweat and tears to help you develop into the beautiful people you are today. They have a vested interest in you and your lives. Thirdly, you're not alone because of me." Maiya pointed to herself.

"Believe it or not, whether I know you by name or not, each of you probably represents a place that I've been," she continued. "And if for that reason in and of itself, I'm with you in this too. Because I know the power of healing and deliverance in Christ Jesus, I am *definitely* in this with you. And you don't have to wait until you're grown or older to receive it. You can have it now."

As she made eye contact with those closest to the front, she saw various eyes filling with tears, males and females alike. She couldn't help but see herself in them.

"So with that said, this is not Prophetess Maiya Jackson standing here before you. I don't want to speak as the accomplished writer, two-time Stellar Award winner or even the Princess of Gospel music," Maiya said, naming a few of her accomplishments to really get her point across. "Now although in reality I'm humbled to have been called all those things, today I want you to see just plain Maiya – a woman who was once you. I don't want you to see what looks like glory without realizing that there is a real story. A real struggle. I was someone that had so many deep-seated secrets, hang-ups, and anything else you can name. Things that almost destroyed my life."

Maiya went on to describe how she was once in their shoes. "I was raped, molested, abandoned, looked down upon, talked about sorely by family, rejected, treated as an outcast and many other things. And yes, I did my share of wrong as well. Please don't get it twisted. All of this pain was not solely because of other people. I was a culprit as well. When I say I did my wrong, baby, I mean I did it. If you can think it, I did it and then some.

I was good at it too. You know when you like something, you tend to be good at it and do it often."

When she was sure that she had their undivided attention, she knew that was the moment to announce the deliverer. God Himself!

"But with God," Maiya continued, not missing a beat as she sensed an undeniable shift in the atmosphere with those three words. "I overcame and here I am now. NOW didn't come easy for me. But I made it to NOW. The real story is in HOW. HOW was even harder. It was harder for many reasons, but mainly because of me."

Have Your way, Lord, Maiya prayed as the atmosphere shifted even more, confirming that she had followed God correctly. That she was on the right track concerning these young people and even the adults.

"Today I'm finally prepared to tell you how. I'm not going to preach to you, but I must, first and foremost tell you that it was mainly by the grace of God that I am standing here today. Things have been done to me and I have done things that probably should have and would have caused my death or at least put me close to it. But thanks be unto God who gives us the victory through Christ Jesus, I can firmly say, I made it and so can you. I know that many of you are wondering exactly what I've been through and I know y'all want to know what I did."

Laughter erupted all over the room. Heads nodded. The crowd looked like they really wanted to know what this seemingly well-put-together woman could possibly have done that was so bad. What they were looking at was the reformed Maiya. They didn't know the old Maiya. Believe that!

"I'll start by telling you that at the age of eight, my uncle begin to molest and rape me every chance he got. He would make me look at pictures of nude people, women having sex with women; men having sex with men; and multiple people having sex with each other. Then he would make me do the things on those pictures. I'm not talking about just a little touching and patting. I'm talking about real sex with a real dirty old man with no teeth, false ones or whatever he had."

It wasn't what Maiya said, but *how* she said that last statement that generated laughter around the room yet again. Even the people on the podium laughed. The animated look on her face only added to the laughter.

That was just Maiya's way. She could insert humor into the most serious moments. Yet despite the laughter, she could see the interest, the connections being made, and the stares of those who couldn't believe someone else knew their treachery and their pain firsthand.

Maiya gripped the podium with both hands and steadied her breathing pattern. The moment of transparency had been fully upon her. There'd been no turning back then.

"This happened until I was twelve years old. It happened often. It hurt. It was scary and it changed me. On top of that, I was forced to live with this secret the whole time, live with this pain that ran deeper than just a physical pain. This pain was the kind of pain that lasted almost a lifetime. Although I'm standing here before you now, please believe me, the pain just subsided recently, like over the past few years."

Maiya realized that she was trembling at that point, so she paused and took a deep breath. She shared with them that this was not something she could just forget and she didn't forgive easily. She knew that unforgiveness was something all of them were likely struggling with for one reason or another. She knew it because of her experiences, not because anyone had specifically told her that. That's why she impressed upon them how necessary forgiveness was to the new lives they embarked upon and their lives afterward.

"Listen to me," Maiya continued. "I forgave when I began to understand the scripture as it pertains to forgiving others so that God will forgive you. When I realized how much I truly needed God to forgive me, I began to reevaluate my decisions on forgiving and forgetting. This is where my escape began. It started with my mindset. Today I want to encourage you to reconsider your thoughts concerning forgiveness. Forgiveness is more about you than it is about the person who wronged you."

Then Maiya proceeded to tell them how she escaped. How it happened in stages. "My grandmother, whom I call Momma, insisted on me moving to Atlanta, Georgia with my birth mother. Now to most of you, that sounds like a good idea and partially, I'll admit that it was. It was good because I got away from Old No-Tooth, his sex books, and the physical abuse. I just couldn't get away from the memories and nightmares. But on the other hand, maybe it wasn't so good after all. My birth mother did not have the spirit of a mother. She was young, too focused on her men and her job to be there for me or my siblings. I was particularly seen as a hindrance in her eyes. So I went from molestation and rape to being alone, unsupervised, and abandoned again. No wonder I became so HOT in the tail. I'm talking hotter than Louisiana and Texas Pete put together. As you all would say, I was off the chain. As a matter of fact, I broke the chain and all its links."

Maiya took another deep breath and continued in a more somber tone. "Besides being hot, I was very angry. I resented my birth mother for not believing me and rescuing me when I told her about the sexual abuse years ago. I resented her even more because once I was back with her, she still wasn't interested in me or my well-being."

The room became cemetery quiet, solemn at the mention of not being believed. Directly in front of Maiya sat a very pretty red-haired young lady, who dropped her head and slumped her shoulders completely over at that exact moment. That part of the message had clearly hit home with the girl.

"Today I see that all I went through was not in vain, because I am more than qualified to tell you that it is not all your fault and you can get through this. If I had to change anything about my life at this point, I'd change nothing because it has made me who I am and prepared me for you today," Maiya continued.

"Secondly, even though my granny played her part in getting me out physically, it was God that got me out emotionally and spiritually. He got me out in the most important way. Because I know that He's God and I know that He's able, I promise you that He can get you out too. We'll talk more about that today, because more importantly than your bodies being out of those situations, your hearts, minds and souls need to be free as well."

As Maiya talked, she couldn't seem to tear her attention away from the red-haired girl, whom she later learned was named Chloe Jordan. There was something extremely familiar about Chloe, about her mannerism. Earlier she'd walked in the room alone with her head down and with great sadness in her eyes. If that message wasn't for anyone else today, it was for *that* girl.

"Now for the questions that still need answers," Maiya continued. "Why didn't anyone stop Old No-Tooth? How did he get away with it at all and for so long? What happened to my birth mother?"

Maiya paused, took another deep breath and then answered those pivotal questions. "I was terrified to tell anyone for years because he made it clear that he would kill me if I did. Back then, death scared me and so I remained quiet for the most part. But I did tell *one* person – my birth mother. I remember it as clearly today as if it were yesterday. When I told her, she called me a liar to my face. If that wasn't enough, she said that if he was doing it, I liked it. That was like a slap in my face. Her reaction told me that she didn't care anything about me. In my young mind, if my own mother didn't care about me that meant nobody else cared either. That also meant that Old No-Tooth would get away with what he'd done to me since nobody cared enough to stop him. Little did I know, he really wouldn't get away with it. God was watching!"

And then it happened. Chloe got up and ran out the room. Only seconds before, she'd trembled in her seat with bloodshot red eyes and a terrified look on her face. Had taking flight been inevitable for her?

CHAPTER FOUR
Redirecting Lives

Maiya paused the message, unable to continue without first making sure someone was with Chloe. She turned and nodded to Angie, who knew exactly what that gesture meant – *Go get her and by any means necessary, bring her back and stay with her.*

Angie wasted no time pursuing Chloe.

Confident that the young lady was in good hands, Maiya returned to her sharing. "Many, many years later Old No-Tooth died a slow and painful death. And you know what, I was glad to see him go. Yet it still didn't take the memories away. On top of that, I found in God's Word that I was charged to esteem others higher than myself. I took that to include those who had wronged me. Even Old No-Tooth! Baby, that was H.A.R.D. Did God really expect me to esteem this person who had done so much harm and wrong to me? Yes. That took a lot of teaching and prayer. It still does. I felt like ain't nobody got time for that!"

Once again there was laughter in the room, yet Maiya's point was not missed. It lightened the air a little after the tense few moments they'd had. She was grateful that she continued to hold their interest because there was so much more to share with them.

"Now for many of you, those same types of responses may be part of the very reason why you have not talked to anyone about the things happening to you or the feelings you have. I came here to encourage you to talk to someone."

As if on cue, Angie walked back into the room with Chloe. Talk about perfect timing! If no one else needed to hear the rest of that message, Chloe did. Maiya knew she had to get through to that particular young woman. Today!

"There is someone who will believe you, who will help you, be there for you and *not* reject you. God has placed in your lives listening ears, caring hearts and people who are moved into action because of love. Love for God and love for you." Maiya looked pointedly toward Chloe and added, "Young ladies and gentleman, you are important to us and I feel confident in saying that the people here love you and want only the best for you. Part of getting the best for you is *your* willingness to communicate. Talking will also help you to get it out. Sometimes you just need to get some things off your chest. *Please, please, please,* don't hold it in. It will eat away at you like a cancerous tumor and it can even kill you. If it doesn't kill you physically, it will surely kill you spiritually, mentally and emotionally."

Maiya spoke from experience. Talking about her past had been the hardest thing to do. She always felt like people were looking down on her when they heard what she'd been through. It made her feel like an outcast. Like she didn't belong, all of which she shared with today's crowd.

"But that's when God stepped in. Once again through His Word, He assured me that not only did I belong in the places He allowed me to go, I belong to Him and the Body of Christ," Maiya said. "I know that's probably a little deep, but what God wants you to know is that you're not an outcast and you're not alone. Scripture says that he that is in Christ Jesus is a new creature, all things are become new and the old things have passed away. All things have passed away – the good and the bad that I did before I decided to make Jesus the Lord of my life. No matter how good of a person I was, it meant nothing without the Blood of Jesus covering me. Even after accepting Christ, I found that it did me no good to hold on to my testimony and keep it to myself as if it were some kind of hidden treasure. I had to talk about it for my healing and for others. So here I am today doing just that."

Maiya walked away from the podium to the front of the stage and sat down. It helped her connect even more with the people in the audience. She saw the interest on their faces, but the hesitancy in their eyes was just as real. She needed them to know that she wasn't talking down at them but rather *to* them, to their hurt and pain.

"Don't let this opportunity that you have to get help, to talk to someone and to change the path of your life, slip away," Maiya continued, letting her heels drop to the floor and her legs swing beneath her. "Grab hold of this chance and don't let go until you get what you need. Even more so I encourage you to do as Christ instructed and take His yoke upon you and learn of Him for His burden is light and His yoke is easy. Simply said, accept Jesus as your personal Savior, learn about Who He is and what He means to your life and allow *Him* to heal you in the unseen places that only you and Him know about. There is nothing too hard for God and surely there is nothing God can't handle."

16

Maiya recognized the Spirit of the Lord working mightily at that time. In another service, in a different arena, she would've been ready to take it to the cross, burial, resurrection and tune it up, all at the same time. But that moment was different. There had been a different kind of anointing resting upon her *and* in that place today. Once again the Spirit of God had just moved her from one level to another as she shared God's Word and her testimony.

Maiya held out her hand toward Angie as she continued to speak. She motioned for her to bring Chloe over. She knew she was taking a chance, because that child had been devastated by someone and something. Yet she could not miss that opportunity to minister to her under that anointing.

"You are bright young men and ladies and this is your time," Maiya said. "The wait is over. The hindrances are gone, the obstacles removed, and the hurt is being healed at this moment as I speak. You are being restored, refreshed and revived. New life comes to you from the Father. It is your time. It's your time to go, do and be whatever you purpose in your heart. From here, the sky really is the limit. The only person that can keep you from reaching your goal is you. God is on your side and with Him you cannot fail. If you have suffered tragedy as I have, talk to someone."

As Chloe finally walked over, Maiya waved her to the stage where she sat and motioned for her to sit next to her. Not ignoring the others in the audience, she put her arms around the girl, looked her in the eye and spoke directly into Chloe's spirit. "You owe it to yourself to release all that pain and anguish and live your life. Live it to the fullest and enjoy it. Live it with God as your guide. Walk with your head up, stop looking down. Baby, forgive yourself, forgive those folks and move on. Loose that stuff and let go."

Maiya still held on to Chloe's trembling frame as she turned back to the crowd, only to find them weeping like little children. *My God what a sight that had been!* Even though she'd spoken directly to Chloe, their spirits had heard her loud and clear as well.

"Jesus told a woman in the Bible that her faith had made her whole and He declared her loosed. Walk in faith today. I decree you whole and loosed. Free in Jesus Christ. And who the Son sets free is free indeed. There are no more chains holding you and you are no longer bound." Maiya squeezed Chloe tighter and added, "Satan has no hold on you and no power over you. You are empowered by Jesus and you can make it."

Then Maiya did something else that she hadn't even thought or planned to do. She said to the crowd, "Come here."

Confused looks settled upon their faces.

"Come here," Maiya reiterated. "Come down to this altar with me, if you want to. I'm not forcing you to. It's not mandatory, but if you will, come here." To her surprise, every child in that room walked toward her.

Even now she was humbled by the memory of so many young people crowding around her.

"Let them come up here. Make room around me, move the podium. Make room for them," Maiya told the administrators in a loving, yet firm tone that was saturated with Godly authority.

People immediately moved the podium. Soon she was surrounded by tears, red eyes, trembling bodies, hurt, and pain. She was also surrounded by healing that waited to be administered. By then their hearts were open to receive it.

"I can't tell you all that I *only* made it by the grace of God. I had to do the work as well, but it took me a lot longer because I would not talk to anyone after that first try," Maiya confessed. "I wouldn't even talk to God and it caused me to have to learn a lot of lessons the hard way. There were times I got hurt because I wouldn't talk. I withheld my testimony for reasons like shame, resentment and worrying about what people would say. If you don't remember anything else I've said to you today, remember this one thing: There is someone somewhere who cares for you. If you can't find that person here, look to God. Go to Him sincerely – in spirit and in truth. Don't even try to sugar coat it or fix it up or make it pretty. He already knows anyway. He is just waiting on you to cast your cares on Him because He does care for you. It was on my knees where I found my best friend. I found the One that would save me, deliver me, restore, refresh, and revive me. He even call me into His ministry. I found the true and living God."

Maiya gave them a tender smile. "Today is your day. Surrender your lives and your hearts to Christ and the rest God will do for you. You only need faith and favor will come to you. Have faith and deliverance will come. Have faith and surely true healing will come. Give it to God today, all of it. He can handle it better than you. He wants you to live the life He has destined for you. My prayer is that you have received the message from the Master today and will now walk into what's already been prepared for you."

Inside Maiya marveled at the fact that as sure as she ministered to their emotions and spirits, once again she'd ministered to her own. That's what she loved so much about God. When He sent her to others; He always sent a message for her too. Today had been about healing and deliverance for them all.

Amazingly, that had been only the tip of the iceberg concerning today's anointed events.

CHAPTER FIVE
Wow! Who Would Have Thought?

Maiya felt warmth spread through her body at the memory of sitting in the midst of those amazing young people. She remembered how receptive they'd been when she asked if she could pray for them. She received a resounding yes!

To that answer, Maiya said, "I just want to pray for your salvation. So if you know that you're ready to receive Christ as your Savior, I'll pray for you. I want to pray for peace for you and healing for your hearts and minds today. Is that all right?"

When she received another resounding yes, she smoothly entered into a Holy Spirit-led prayer. Once the prayer was over, Maiya brought her message to a satisfied end. She knew she'd said everything God wanted her to say. Done everything she was supposed to do.

Upon standing, she hugged Chloe and several others. Then she allowed them to return to their seats.

Tears streamed down Maiya's face as she finally took her own seat. Through her tears she could see the young people crying also. Many stood to their feet and gave her a standing ovation that lasted over five minutes. Truthfully that applause wasn't really for her, but surely for the God that stood up in her.

Just as reverently as they'd stood, the young people fell to the floor on their faces in reverence to God. There was wailing and sincere pleas for Him to take control heard all over the building. On the podium, even more chairs had to be moved out of the way because they were all shouting.

What a mighty move of God!

Lord, thank You for helping me get Your point across, Maiya thought, convinced that none of this had been about her. *I made it on my knees, just*

You and I. And I know even today I'm still not worthy.

Looking back now, who would have ever imagined her being where she was today? Nobody. Least of all her.

Glory! Maiya praised, still so in awe of God. The little girl who loved music and writing, who they said would never become anything, turned out to be something after all.

Look at God! How about that? Won't He do it!

At that point, Maiya couldn't keep her praise to herself any longer. She burst forth in the signature praise dance that she was known for. A dance for God that had been birthed in the privacy of her bedroom and bathroom – her personal sanctuaries. This dance wasn't for show, but rather to glorify God.

Angie quickly positioned herself nearby along with other members of their team. As they went forth in praise, they kept a watchful eye on Maiya. That kind of genuine love and concern made her appreciate them even more.

When things finally calmed down and the tears in the room turned to sniffles, Star took the podium. She wiped her eyes clear and just smiled at everyone, especially Maiya. She kept opening and closing her mouth but no words came out.

"I'm speechless," Star said when she was finally able to talk again. "Some of the things you all heard today, I'm just now learning as well. Furthermore, I've never moved so fast in my life. It was like the Holy Spirit swept me up in a whirlwind and then gently let me down today."

Maiya smiled and nodded. She'd felt that way herself today.

"This has been an amazing experience and I believe I can safely say that it will never be forgotten by any of us," Star concluded through a steady stream of tears. Still somewhat choked up, she dismissed the teenagers and wished them well.

As the youth left the auditorium, Maiya talked briefly with Star. As always, the conversation was uplifting.

"Thank you so much for coming today. You are even more amazing than I thought before you got here," Star said, hugging her a little tighter than usual. "Girl, I can't believe that we lived in the same house all those years and I never knew this stuff. I must confess, all that time it seemed like you just had some childish issues. Now I realize you had issues from your childhood. That's a major difference. Now I understand you more than I ever did, Maiya. That's a lesson I'm going to be sure to teach the kids – sometimes it's not what you think!"

"Star, you loved me the best way you could back then and regardless of what you thought, you didn't give up on me," Maiya replied. "It's all water under the bridge. Besides, I owe it all to God. We live and learn and we have done both." She hugged her again. "Thank you for having me, I will be back soon. I think I'd like to do a roundtable talk with some of them so they can ask questions and things like that. How long do we have until they exit the program? Please make sure that my number is given to any of them that want it. I'm available. I made the promise to God that I would be available for His use and available to His people." Maiya spoke in a rush of words, not bothering to wait for a response in her excitement to minister to the teenagers on a more one-on-one basis.

"See that's what I mean." Star chuckled and shook her head. Awe and admiration were in her eyes. "You just finished doing one thing and already that mind of yours is working on the next thing. I'll have to check the dates and we'll work it out for you to come back soon. I already know some of them are definitely going to want to talk to you, so get ready for the calls, especially from Chloe. I believe you got through to her today. When she was sitting next to you, I saw a peace in her that I haven't seen since she's been here."

Maiya smiled at her. "Chloe will be fine. God has His hand on her. We can't give up now. The Lord has brought us all too far."

Star walked with her toward the back exit, making loud click-clack noises with her stylish gold heels. Though her feet were small, they were just as robust as the rest of her petite frame.

Lord, she's definitely a force to be reckoned with even if she is so small, Maiya prayed as they walked together. *Her physical body might be a size two, but her heart and soul are larger than life.* No one cared so unselfishly, shared so easily and forgave so diligently as Star. She was definitely one of a kind and in a league of her own.

Maiya thanked God for their friendship. She was especially grateful that Star was a lifetime friend and not just a seasonal one.

When they got to the exit door of the auditorium, Maiya noticed that Angie had brought the car around. What a blessing her assistant was! Like God, she was always on time...or at least always tried to be.

Maiya hugged Star one last time before leaving. Then she entered the passenger side of the purple Lexus ES 460 – an additional blessing from God. It was time to go home to yet another blessing. It was also time to prepare for her first ministry opportunity at a national conference with Bishop Horton and many other great men and women of God.

CHAPTER SIX
Blessed to Be a Blessing

Whew! What a life – the good times and the bad, Maiya thought, shaking herself back to reality as they entered her gated community.

Looking down at her purple-faced Rolex, she realized she'd been in a daze for the last twenty minutes. She was glad that Angie understood her so well. Otherwise she might run the risk of offending her every time she faded out like that.

As they pulled into the garage of her eight-bedroom home, Maiya couldn't help but feel a little giddy. The house and everything in it were additional blessings from God.

Some folks chided her for having eight bedrooms. Well, she served a big God and she liked big things. The way Maiya saw it, Heaven was surely bigger than the house she had and she was definitely going to reside there someday. Besides, somebody might need somewhere to stay for a while. Why not with her?

Truthfully, Maiya opened her doors when necessary to help others even when she didn't have eight bedrooms. She wasn't about to stop doing it now. She knew she couldn't afford to stop after all God had done for her.

"Angie, thank you for driving me today," Maiya told her assistant as they came to a stop in her left side garage. The other team members had already gone home. "Please take the rest of the day off. You need some rest. You've been on the road with me for the last four weeks. We have big things coming up soon, so I want you good and rested. Do you need anything before you go?" She always tried to be a good employer. The well-being of those who served with her was of the utmost importance.

"No, I'm fine." Angie smiled at her considerate words. "You should get some rest too. You have been going non-stop as well. Preaching, teaching, and singing. Girl, I don't know how you do it." She paused and quickly added, "I know, I know, by the grace of God and you stay on your knees."

They laughed out loud together.

"You got it, girl. That's where I'm headed now – to my secret closet to get on my knees and then to my bed to get some sleep," Maiya said.

"Well, I have a few stops to make and then I'll be going home too," Angie replied, turning off the car. "Once again, *please* get some rest. You are not superwoman," she chided in a drill-sergeant like tone. "And as always, I'll be praying for you."

"Yes, ma'am," Maiya said, loving Angie even more for caring so genuinely and taking such good care of her. Truly God had shown them His undeniable favor when He blessed them with each other.

Although Angie was her assistant and employee, she was so much more than that. Maiya deemed her a treasured and true friend/sister.

Their friendship budded while they were working regular jobs. Maiya was Angie's supervisor back then. They quickly discovered that they were alike in a lot of ways. Both believed in getting the job done and doing it well. They also shared a belief in Christ and in living a righteous life.

Truth be told, Maiya was the Queen of Cut-Up at times. The Lord put Angie there to help her stay on track. Though that probably seemed backwards, it wasn't. It was just God working in His own special way unbeknown to them at the time.

Ironically, Angie didn't even like Maiya at first. She was standoffish, constantly trying to feel her out until she realized that they had more similarities than differences.

Maiya appreciated the fact that even before they developed a rapport, Angie showed her respect in the little things. Things like coming to work on time and completing her work without complaining. As a result, she seldom had to correct or reprimand her. The rare times she did, Angie took the correction like a champ and turned it around for her good. Now that is a good employee and an even better friend any day!

Because of the way their relationship began and grew, they now worked almost flawlessly together in ministry. Each one in her perspective place, complimenting one another as they went about God's business.

After leaving Maiya's car parked in this garage, Angie went to the right side garage to retrieve her own vehicle – a champagne-colored, Mercedes Benz GLK350. That car was C.L.E.A.N! It had a champagne exterior, peanut butter leather interior complete with every bell, whistle, navigation system and anything else one could ask for. The best part of all – it was paid in full!

That car had been a gift from Maiya. Talk about the blessings of God making rich and adding no sorrow. Talk about blessed to be a blessing.

The most fascinating and laughable thing about Angie's car was the fact that she was driving it at all. She didn't get her driver's license until around 2005. She'd come a long way since then. So much so that Maiya trusted her with her own life on the road.

Angie's house was yet another blessing. Maiya was adamant about making sure that those who diligently served with her didn't have to worry about where they lived, certainly not Angie. Again, she'd been blessed to be a blessing to someone so obviously deserving.

Although tangible things like that didn't worry Maiya, she was always very mindful of them when it came to her staff. After working in the County Office of Family and Children Services, she knew what making little to nothing was like. Both she and Angie lived through the days of trying to make ends meet and care for their children among other things. It's amazing they were able to keep a level head and maintain their sanity during those lean years.

To not have those worries now was an added blessing. The peace of mind alone made Maiya feel rich beyond compare. The money didn't bring this peace. God did it, making them rich in more ways than one!

Waving goodbye to Angie as she drove away, Maiya closed the garage door and entered the house fully. She breathed deeply, happy to finally be home for some rest and relaxation. Walking through the family room, she recognized that all too familiar twinge in her spirit when something wasn't quite right.

Maybe I'm still so sensitive from today's powerful encounter, Maiya thought, partially dismissing that twinge as she made her way up the back stairs. *If I'm still picking up things in my spirit, then yes, I really do need to rest.*

CHAPTER SEVEN
Calm before the Storm

Upstairs, Maiya changed into a long satin nightshirt, turned her cell phone off, and then spent some much needed private time in the presence of the Lord. When she was done praying, she turned her cell phone back on and carried it downstairs with her. She headed straight to the kitchen for her favorite drink – an ice cold Dr. Pepper, complete with the slush effect.

She pulled a glass from the shelf above the sink and then sat at the kitchen island to pour her drink. Sliding the tall bar stool away from the counter, she sat quietly and sipped, relishing the peace of home.

It was summertime. Her children were out of town with their father's family. She'd been on the move since they left. She was grateful to finally have a moment to just sit down and relax.

Maiya smiled as she looked around her custom made kitchen. She planned every detail of it from the brown and black marble mixed countertops to the oak wood drawers. God sent the money to bring that vision to pass.

Thanks for being Who You are in my life and for how You've changed my life, Maiya prayed. She was even more thankful that God allowed her to make an impact in the lives of others.

She smiled wider as snippets from today's conference came flooding back. *Special thanks for how You changed Chloe's life among so many others today.*

As a yawn worked its way out of her mouth in between sips of soda, she realized that it was time to go back upstairs. This time for sleep.

Her cell phone rang just as she rose from the stool. The number registered from her most favorite man on this earth. Her husband – Napoleon.

Napoleon was actually Maiya's third husband. Husband Number One gave her two beautiful children and lots of drama. Husband Number Two gave her bumps and bruises. She wisely freed herself of them both. She hoped to go the distance with her current husband.

A minister of the Gospel as well, Napoleon had been preaching revivals for the last few weeks. Since both of them were traveling more with their ministries, they had not shared their usual alone time. This was the first time they had been separated for more than a few days. It was new to them, but they decided it was what God would have them to do.

Maiya was doing her part to be obedient to God. Napoleon said he was doing his part. She would continue to take him at his word...until he gave her cause to do otherwise.

Marriage to Napoleon was like a dream come true. Maiya often said that it was more than out of this world and just short of heavenly.

"Hey, baby," Napoleon said when she picked up the phone.

"Hey, love," Maiya replied, unable to stop smiling. It was more than sweet music to her ears to hear his deep satiny voice.

"I miss you, woman." He sounded nearer for some reason.

"I miss you too."

"Well, get up here and show me how much." He suddenly appeared at the top of the spiral staircase.

"What?" She yanked her head upward. "Boy, what are you..." Her words trailed off when she saw him up there, looking as handsome as the day they met. She dropped her phone and bounced up the stairs two at a time into the arms of her beloved husband.

They held each other for several long precious moments, relishing the solace of being in each other's presence again. Time seemed to stand still for Maiya in this man's embrace. She loved the feel of his arms around her and his breath upon her neck.

Napoleon was well missed and she didn't mind showing him how much. *This*...the solace...was well missed too. That solace started out with a forever promise. Would their forever be the way she imagined it? She hoped so.

Standing eye level with her husband, Maiya returned Napoleon's kisses as he picked her up in his strong arms and drew her closer. She shivered at his touch. Oh how she missed his skillful hands over the past few weeks.

His lips captured hers again in a tender, yet very seductive kiss. Time seemed to stand still once more. Any longer and the hallway would have surely spun.

Napoleon carried Maiya to their master bathroom effortlessly, as if she weighed nothing at all. "Close your eyes. Close your eyes," he said the closer they got to the bedroom door.

"What are you up to?" Maiya was intrigued. Her giggle was suppressed, but she couldn't hide her wide smile. She loved surprises and Napoleon could always come up with the best ones.

"Just close your eyes and you'll see." He was such a charmer.

"Okay, okay," Maiya conceded, ignoring that check in her spirit about how deceitful charm could be at times. Rather she focused on how her husband had come up with yet another way to wow her, show his professed love, and keep the romance strong between them. She gladly covered her face with her hands, not realizing how often she did that in other areas of their relationship.

Once they entered the bedroom, she felt another unction in her spirit that made her pause. Yet because she wanted to just enjoy that time with Napoleon, she didn't mention it or dwell on it. She pledged her life, heart, love and her body to this man and this one only. She was 'all in' as some people would say.

Some friends teased her, declaring that she was the picture of 'Fully Committed'. Maiya simply shrugged it off. She knew she was loyal, often times to a fault.

"Okay, open your eyes," Napoleon said after placing her upon her feet in the bathroom.

Maiya uncovered her face and saw the nice hot bubble bath that he prepared. He used his favorite scent – cucumber melon, her favorite flowers – calla lilies, and the cucumber melon scented candles they both equally enjoyed.

Another smile spread across her lips, stretching all the way up to her eyes. She took in the sheer beauty of the love expressed to her from the man she promised her endless love to.

"Oh, baby. Thank you so much," Maiya said, removing her purple nightshirt. Although she loved his display of love, she just couldn't shake that lingering feeling of uneasiness in her spirit. She knew better than to dismiss it completely. She knew it would have to be addressed at some point.

Maiya looked intently at Napoleon, trying to discern the reason for that feeling she knew all too well. *What is it, Lord?*

"Now I know you are coming in here with me," she said aloud, careful not to give her thoughts away. "Don't even think of saying no. I'll pull you in here if I have to." She chuckled, lowering herself into the Jacuzzi tub.

Laughing with her, Napoleon readily complied with her request as he disrobed and slid behind her. Once he was settled, she rested her back against his broad chest and sighed in contentment. He used that moment to run his hands across her silky skin, touching her here, there...everywhere.

Maiya welcomed that non-verbal communication and returned his caresses. Together they closed the door on the last few weeks apart and again consummated their love in the sanction of wedded bliss. All was well...for now.

CHAPTER EIGHT
One-on-One Ministry

After spending quality time with Napoleon, enjoying more rest and time in prayer, Maiya felt like she could tackle the world and more the next day. She was ecstatic, so excited about everything. She looked forward to her upcoming trips and the planning sessions that were scheduled with her team. There were event and conference details that needed to be worked out. She couldn't wait to share the new ideas that God had given her recently.

Overall, Maiya was just elated with life as a whole and very thankful that things were as good as they were, especially when it came to her marriage. Although she and Napoleon shared great times now, their marriage had been challenged before. There were struggles that they'd gotten through with love, counseling and some serious forgiveness.

Thanks be unto God, they made it through the rough patches with the various mothers of his children. The women weren't all receptive of Maiya's relationship with their kids at first. Once they realized that she only wanted what was best for them, which was for all the adults to come together for the good of the children, they eventually came around.

Napoleon's infidelity was a lot harder to work through. Maiya was ready to call it quits as soon as she found out. She'd been down that road before and was absolutely not about to travel that route again with anyone. However, she learned that marriage was hard work and she believed theirs was worth the effort.

It had taken a lot out of Maiya to forgive Napoleon, but he assured her that those challenging days were completely over. Along with her forgiveness, she decided to take him at his word so that both of them could move forward and live out their lives the way God intended.

Preparing to get her day started on that bright sunny Monday, Maiya grabbed her clothes from the closet and headed to the bathroom. Napoleon had already left the house since he had business meetings of his own today.

As she showered, she sang one of her favorite original songs – *Cover Me*. That song was very special to her. It was the song that ministered to her during some of the difficult moments between her and Napoleon as well as other trials of life. It was her song of petition and praise.

Continuing to sing, Maiya stepped out the shower just as the phone ring. She recognized the ringtone as that of her ministry line. She quickly wrapped a plush purple and white towel around herself and dashed into her bedroom to retrieve the phone. She barely made it before the last ring.

"Hello, this is Prophetess Maiya, how may I help you?" she said, trying not to sound too winded.

Whew! I have got to get in better shape, she thought, attempting to catch her breath.

"Hello, my name is Charlene Baker," the woman on the phone frantically gushed out. "I'm a member of Northridge Prophetic Center. I was there when you came to speak at our women's conference last month. You talked to us about being free in Christ and about not letting anyone take away the freedom that God had given us." She sounded utterly distraught the more she spoke.

Maiya's spiritual antennas instantly went up the way they always did when it was time to minister, especially one-on-one. As the woman's name jogged her memory, she mentally thumbed through more memory files and pulled up additional information about her.

Charlene was a twenty-six-year-old minister from Norfolk, Indiana. She was a fairly strong-minded woman, married, but with no children. About 5'4, she had long black hair, mahogany skin, and weighed around a hundred and forty-five pounds. She was a very pretty woman, but unfortunately, her self-esteem wasn't quite as stunning. She lacked confidence and from what Maiya was being told now, she was in an abusive relationship.

"I need your help please," Charlene continued through her tears. "I can't take it anymore. This man is threatening to kill me. He's saying I can't go to church. He's saying that I can't preach anymore and that he's going to leave if I keep going to church. He calls me French whores if I put on makeup and perfume. Today, he threw cooking oil on me to keep me from going to work. Please, *please* help me! I don't know where else to turn. I can't go to my church. They'll just talk about me. I can't tell my family. They won't care. Please, please, *please*! I have to do something. I don't want to die."

Maiya sat down at her vanity table and listened intently to what Charlene said and didn't say. She remained silent and prayerful as the woman finally stopped talking and just cried for a few moments.

"Charlene before we talk further, let's pray," Maiya said as the woman's cries turned to sniffles.

"Okay," Charlene replied. Her voice was barely audible now.

"Father, in Jesus Name, we thank You for who You are and how You are. We thank You for this moment right now because we know that You ordained it. Father, allow both of us to hear from You clearly and receive what You have for Your daughter at this time. Thank You that You're all knowing and every answer that she needs is in You. We bless You and we love You. In Jesus Name we pray. Amen."

"Amen." Charlene sounded just a tad bit louder and clearer this time.

Now that Maiya had formally involved God in the situation, she gained the liberty to do even more multitasking. Quickly drying off, she walked back into the bathroom and put her earpiece in so that she could continue to talk while getting dressed.

"Charlene, I'd like to first tell you that Jesus loves you so very much," Maiya said. "And although you're in a rough time, you can't give up now. I'd like to ask you a question if you don't mind."

"That's fine," Charlene quietly replied.

"What do you want to do?"

"What do you mean?" Charlene sounded confused by that question.

Maiya intentionally asked her an open-ended question so she would not be tempted to answer with a yes or no only. "You asked me to help you. You said you don't want to die. I need to know what you want to do. What are you asking God to help you with and to do for you?"

A few moments of silence passed.

"I want to kill him," Charlene replied, sounding just as enraged as she'd been distraught earlier. "I'm tired of being called out of my name and today he slapped me on the floor. That is my last straw. I will not tolerate anyone putting their hands on me. So you want to know what I want to do, I want to kill him. I want to kill everything in him like he's been killing things in me."

Maiya could hear the grinding of the woman's teeth as she listened quietly to her tirade. Charlene needed to release this anger now before her thoughts became actions. While the tirade continued, she finished getting dressed and sent a text message to Angie.

"I was a preacher when he married me and I'm going to be one when he leaves," Charlene continued. "I don't know where he gets off thinking he can change who I am. I can't believe I didn't see this coming. I'll tell you this though; I will *not* be stupid again. I'm getting out of this."

"Charlene, let's deal with this first," Maiya said, jumping back into the conversation. "You can't kill him. Well, you can, but it won't solve your problem."

"He *is* my problem," she replied.

"No," Maiya responded, "He is *a* problem. I need you to hear me out as I'm hearing God. Your problem is that you've allowed someone to be in the position that God should be in. Now that person has turned around and hurt you. You're angry, not just with him, but with the world. This incident with your husband has pushed you over the edge. You have every right to be mad with him for hitting you and calling you out of your name, but killing him isn't going to kill what's going on in you. I can't tell you what to do concerning your marriage and whether you choose to stay or go. That's completely between you and God. He will tell you how to handle it. I can, however, help you deal with *you*."

"I called you because I want to know what to do about this man, *not* me." Charlene was almost whining now. She sounded defeated.

"Daughter, you can't do anything about that man. He has his own will. But you can do something about *you*. If I were talking to him, I'd tell him the same thing."

"Well, why do you think there's something wrong with me? I'm a good wife. I do what I'm supposed to at home, I work and I pay all the bills. I cook. I clean. I don't understand why this is about me," Charlene said as her anger level rose once again.

By now, Maiya was in the car heading to her first meeting of the day. Her whole team was scheduled to be there as well. Angie knew to go ahead and delegate someone to lead prayer if Maiya wasn't in the room at start time. Talk about a great assistant!

Knowing that Angie would hold the meeting down until she got there, Maiya was able to keep her current focus on Charlene. She knew she couldn't give this young lady all the answers in one conversation. But she would help her as much as she could, even if it meant simply planting seeds for her to ponder and hopefully grow later on.

"Charlene, I didn't say anything was wrong with you or that you aren't a good wife," Maiya replied. "I'm saying that you've got things that have been building up in you that started long before he came into the picture. He just happened to agitate those things and now what's in you is surfacing. That's not a bad thing. It just means that it's time for you and God to deal with them. You said you want me to help you. I want to do just that – help you."

"I'm ready to receive help," Charlene said humbly.

"Good, so let's just cut to the chase," Maiya replied. "You're harboring unforgiveness and while you feel like you want to kill him, it's actually killing you. It's hindering you. I don't know where it's all stemming from, but you do. The first thing you need to do to help yourself is acknowledge that. You don't have to tell me who it is or what happened. But for your own sake, you have to admit that not only are you mad with him, you're mad with other people too. There is absolutely nothing wrong with admitting to yourself that there are some things you haven't gotten over yet."

"He reminds me of my past," Charlene blurted out. "The things he says make me feel just like I did back then. I feel like nothing. I was never good enough, never pretty enough for the people in my life. All I ever heard was that I was black and ugly and that I couldn't do anything right." She sounded defeated all over again.

Throughout that lengthy conversation, Maiya heard anger, defeat, sadness, hurt, disappointment and depression. Now they were finally getting to the underlying source of all that Charlene felt.

"Why don't we start with your past," Maiya suggested. "It's time to release the old hurts because you can't effectively make good decisions for your life now or your future, if you're judging them by the past. The truth of the matter is, whatever happened then is real. You were hurt by it. It negatively affected your view of yourself. So I need you to do an exercise for me," she said, turning into the parking lot of the conference center where the meeting was being held. As she waited for an answer from Charlene, she drove around and looked for an available parking spot.

"Okay," Charlene finally replied after some thought.

"Write down everything that was done to you in the past and the person who did it to you," Maiya said. "Then during your daily prayers, ask God to heal you of those hurts and to help you to forgive them by faith. It's not an overnight process, but through prayer, God will begin to reverse the effects of what they did and said. You just have to believe that God is able to help you. This is a process, so I don't want you to feel like I'm not helping you with your issue. Yet this is how God is leading me and what He wants is for you to be whole. Whether you are with this man or not, your wholeness and healing is God's priority."

"I didn't realize we would be talking about this when I called you, but I guess I do need to deal with it." Charlene sounded much calmer now. "I don't think I knew I was still mad about my past until now. Thank you, Prophetess Maiya. At least I won't kill him now, but I'm *not* staying with him," she added, speaking in full voice.

"Well, that's a decision you have to make with God. But I am going to say this concerning the abuse – get to a safe place. I mean a *physically* safe place. I don't condone abuse of any kind and until he gets some help and you can decide what you're going to do, you need to be safe," Maiya said, parking the car. She continued to sit inside, unwilling to move until God released her from this particular conversation for the time being.

"I will," Charlene replied. "I don't know what to do about him, but I know I can't live like this. Thank you for taking time to talk to me today. I know you're probably extremely busy. I apologize for bombarding you with all this."

"No, ma'am," Maiya said, "I am *never* too busy for this. It is important that we learn to care for one another whether it is in word or deed, but definitely in deed. Sometimes we just need a listening ear. I am very happy that we had a chance to talk. I'd like to talk with you again, if you don't mind."

"Yes, I'd like that. I have a feeling I'm going to need some help dealing with these past issues. Even though I heard what you said, I just don't know if I can do it right," Charlene said.

"There is no right or wrong way to heal. The process is different for each person. The final objective is the same – to heal. I'll have my assistant Angie to call you and set up another time for us to talk."

"Thank you. I really do appreciate it. Can we pray again before we get off the phone?" Charlene asked.

"Not a problem. Let us pray...Father, we thank You again for Your great wisdom and Your power. Thank You that You love us so much that Your desire for us is to be whole and to lack nothing. I pray for my sister Minister Charlene and ask You to guide her through this process of healing and forgiveness. Please uncover any areas that would hinder her. Give her the strength to let go of the old hurts and embrace the future You have for her. Strengthen her mind, her heart, and her spirit and shield them against any ungodly source that would rise up against them. You are an awesome God. You're mighty in all that You do and we thank You in advance that everything she's endured, even the present situation, is working for her good. We love You, we bless You, and we thank You in Jesus Name. Amen," Maiya said, bringing the prayer to a satisfied end. She felt the presence of the Lord and the calm that He always brought. She was grateful for His covering.

"Thank you so much," Charlene said. She started crying again, but this time she was much calmer.

Maiya hoped that calmness meant that she felt the presence of God as well. "You're welcome. I'll talk with you again soon."

After they said their goodbyes, Maiya put her phone in her purse and prepared to join her team inside the building for today's very important meeting. Upon exiting the vehicle, she glanced into the rearview window and saw what looked like Napoleon's car parked two rows back. She was almost positive that was his black Cadillac XTS.

Hmmm, that's interesting. I didn't know he was coming today, Maiya pondered. Napoleon wasn't one of her employees, but as her husband, he often played an active part in her ministry and thus was free to attend all meetings.

Oh well, time to go make some things happen, she thought, pushing those ponderings aside as she locked the car door behind herself.

CHAPTER NINE
The Run In

As Maiya walked toward the building with her black purse and notebook in hand, she rechecked her appearance in the long paneled windows. She wanted to make sure all that multitasking from earlier today hadn't affected her ability to walk in excellence when it came to her attire.

God is good, Maiya thought, carefully perusing her reflection in the row of windows, grateful that she hadn't missed a beat with her appearance today.

Her black wide-legged slacks, white top trimmed in black, and 4" black and white stilettos were on point, giving her a relaxed and yet classy look. Diamond studded black hoops with a matching necklace and ring accompanied the outfit. To complete the look, she wore a signature purple flower in her hair.

After receiving a text from Angie declaring that the meeting was about to start, Maiya picked up her pace upon entering the building. She walked comfortably, yet swiftly in her stilettos. High-heeled shoes were her friends and she was well acquainted with them.

Maiya looked around the Atlanta Conference Center and Suites as she walked toward the guest services desk. The building was exquisite, inside and out. The atmosphere was very serene. The paintings and sconces on the wall were well-placed, giving the building an overall comfortable feel. What a great place to meet today!

"Good morning, I'm here for an 11am meeting in the Victory Room." Maiya smiled at the curly-haired gentleman behind the desk.

"It's the second room to the right," he replied, sounding distracted. He didn't even bother to look up as he pointed in the direction just past the elevators.

"Thank you," Maiya said and then walked away from the desk.

Interesting, she thought, briefly glancing back over her left shoulder at the man.

Now looking forward to what was ahead of her, Maiya felt excitement bubble in her belly the closer she got to the Victory Room. Pausing just outside the door bearing a sign that read '*Reserved – Living With More Ministries*' in fancy calligraphy, she took a deep breath and then walked into the room.

Inside everyone had their heads bowed as Van Taylor, the motivational team lead, prayed. Van was 5'11 with dark cocoa brown skin and a gorgeous smile. He was eloquently spoken and was a longtime friend of Maiya's. Most people thought they were either married, involved or would be because they were so close and protective of one another.

People couldn't seem to grasp the fact that men and women could be good friends without being romantically involved. Yet that was exactly how things were between Maiya and Van. Van was happily married with a son. Happily married as in, in love with his *own* wife, Janine, and not someone else's.

An aspiring motivational speaker, Van used to work in retail before he joined Maiya's ministry. There were many days that he encouraged her in the Word of God and helped to keep her motivated. She believed in him completely, which was why he led that particular part of the ministry. This way even more people could be blessed by his gift.

Maiya knew that Van was destined for greatness, that one day he'd have to leave her ministry and venture out into what God called him to. Until then, she was grateful to have him working with them and she would continue to help him as much as she could.

Standing at the door while Van prayed, Maiya glanced around the room in search of her husband. Napoleon was nowhere to be found.

Where is he? she thought, one hundred percent sure that she'd seen his car outside. It was hard not to miss a custom made vehicle like his.

Brushing that thought to the side for the time being, Maiya returned her focus to Van's prayer. When it ended, she quickly joined the group of seven at the table. She took a brief moment to greet each Vision Team Member with a hug as she made her way to the empty seat next to Angie.

The Vision Team consisted of Angie, Van, Jasmine King, Allysa Day, Maria Phillips, Vickie Simpson, and Kymberli Mathis. Everyone had smiles on their faces.

Those smiles pleased Maiya. She was thankful for the growth of the ministry and for every person that was so willing to work the vision God had given her. They were a faithful group of people. So far they all seemed to be there for more than just a paycheck.

"So sorry I'm late. I had a call that I had to finish before coming in," Maiya explained, settling into her seat. "How is everyone? You look so happy!" She smiled from ear to ear as she looked around the table.

Everyone responded individually. Some said they were great. Others exclaimed their excitement. Angie and Van were quiet. Too quiet. Maiya picked up on that immediately.

Although Angie and Van did respond to her, she knew something was going on by the *way* they responded. They never just nodded to her in greeting. She would talk to them after the meeting. Right now it was time for business.

"So let's recap the last meeting and then we need to discuss our plans for the national conference I'm going to in a few months. Plus I have some ideas I want you all to hear and consider," Maiya said, opening the floor up for discussion. "So who's going first?" Her growling stomach reminded her that she hadn't eaten breakfast, so she grabbed some grapes from the fruit tray on the table and ate while she waited for her team to respond.

Angie jumped right in. "During the last meeting, we listed the goals for our conference which were to secure a facility, set the dates and bring a list of suggested speakers to this meeting. We also talked about music ministry and possibly having a comedian as well."

"We also discussed the motivational moments you want us to have," Van interjected. "We think it's a good idea that they are either at the beginning of the worship experience to help set the tone even further or at the end to close out and summarize the night."

"Well, I think that before we go on to planning these conferences and other great events you have ideas for, we should address how the media might come after *you* personally," Allysa said, nonchalantly running manicured nails through her silky brown and black hair. Her brass tone instantly rubbed everyone the wrong way and caused eyebrows to slightly lift.

Allysa was the newest team member, only twenty-three years old, and fresh out of college. At that age she thought she knew everything. Although she was highly sought after because of her extensive social media marketing skills, her maturity level left something to be desired at times.

Maiya prayed that the influence of this group would be beneficial to Allysa. Fortunately nothing was too hard for God, because the likelihood of them rubbing off on this particular young lady didn't look too good at the moment.

With just a few words, Allysa had gotten off on the wrong foot with this very family-oriented and protective group of people. Almost everyone at the table was in an uproar and immediately had something to say in response. Everyone except for Maiya, Angie, and Van. The latter two looked at Allysa, but didn't say a word.

"This isn't personal, Allysa. This is ministry," Maiya said, promptly bringing order back into the room. "I may share some of my personal life for ministry purposes, but I can assure you, we can handle the media. Yet for the sake of discussion, what's your concern?" She would hear the girl out and also use this moment for training purposes.

"I'm just saying, you've been married three times, divorced twice, and your current husband travels all over this country without you because you're too busy doing other things," Allysa replied. "Don't you think that will raise some questions on the stability of your marriage? Don't you think people might question whether *you* should be holding these 'empowerment conferences' and 'marriage seminars' at all? I just think people will want to know how a person who has been married that many times can really tell anyone about marriage."

"Maiya isn't a marriage counselor and never once has ever claimed to be," Angie said with a definitive edge in her voice. "I don't know where you've been, but Maiya preaches and teaches straight Word. That's how she can tell anybody about anything. She gives them the Word!"

Allysa smirked and shrugged. "Okay, don't deal with it and see what happens. I suggest we get some statements ready, because you never know what's lurking around the corner."

Maiya felt another quickening in her spirit. Remaining silent, she watched the conversation play out a little longer, observing everyone's body language as well. People were starting to tense up and fold their arms across their chests.

"All right, that's enough," Maiya finally said, sensing that it was time to end this particular conversation. "Everyone who has been on this team a while already knows we've dealt with those very questions before, so of course we're not concerned with that. However, Allysa makes a good point, we *should* always be ready. There is something else I want all of you to learn from this and I want you to get it now. Just because the enemy attacks, doesn't mean we have to respond. People can question us, our validity, our qualifications, and so on. This is what you must be secure in. Questioning us or me doesn't make what God has already said about us invalid. It actually strengthens it, because the enemy only attacks those things and people that are a threat to him. Y'all understand?"

"Yes, ma'am," was their united response...except for Allysa, who remained indifferent.

Oh she can be Judas if she wants to. There is an expected end for that foolishness, Maiya thought, making a notation in her notebook to meet with Allysa one-on-one soon. She would not allow dissension within her group. She cared too much about them as people to allow them or their hard work to be undermined by negativity.

"All right, let's move on," Maiya said, promptly changing the subject. "Angie, who are the artists that you have on the list? Y'all know I said I want local people. We have to sow some seeds into them. Help push them into the world's view."

"The first one is Lonnie, she has that new single coming out. The other one is Mr. Griffin. He's that Christian hip-hop artist you love. I have contacted both of them and they are ready. We just need to give them dates and times, which I told them should be set very soon. I have their fee schedules attached to this report and I also emailed them to you," Angie quickly rattled off with excitement in her voice.

Maiya nodded her approval. "That's good, Angie. I love the variety of genres that you've chosen. It's perfect." Then she turned to Van. "What's going on with the motivational speaker?"

"I have two for you to choose from," Van said. "Both are national public speakers. I think either would be a good choice. They are both Christian and they use the Bible as their basis."

Maiya was quiet for a few seconds, waiting as more divine direction settled in her spirit. Finally she said, "Van, your choices are a no. I know the speakers on your list are really good, but I don't want anyone else to do the motivational moment at this conference except *you*. We've already had other people before, but now it's time for you to make it happen. You have everything in you to do it. You're more than capable and most importantly, you're *called* to this. This is a lesson for all of us. You must believe in you. That's where it starts. I think everyone at this table will agree with me that this very special motivational moment should be done by you. That you've been in the background long enough. That it's time for you to come out of hiding."

Everybody in the room started clapping. The words, "I told you so," spilled from many lips. Laughter ensued.

Maiya was glad to know that they saw what she saw in Van.

"Okay, I guess I'm doing it then." Van laughed, crumpling up his paper full of notes now that the matter was settled.

Maiya smiled heartily, feeling so encouraged. It was time to move this meeting even further along. "Let's talk about location now. That's our biggest challenge. I know you all have been working so diligently on finding the right place. We all have. I've seen all of your emails and text messages with attached pictures, so I know there are many great places to choose from. What are your top picks?" She looked around the table as she spoke.

The room suddenly grew quiet.

"What?" Maiya lifted her left brow. "I know y'all are not quiet now with all the stuff that you've sent me. Not to mention the ones I found too. Between all of us, I know something had to stand out."

Finally someone else spoke up. It was Jasmine. She sang with the worship team – *Grace*. Jasmine was a beautiful and intelligent young lady. She was full of love and laughter, always shared unselfishly with everyone, and was favored among the team. She was also never late. Like Maiya,

Jasmine was always straight to the point.

"Listen, we have a surprise for you and you just gotta trust us," Jasmine said. "We have researched, talked to people, and visited the site. We found the perfect place. It's got everything we need – beautiful open conference rooms with great sound systems, bathrooms close by and it's got a hotel attached so people don't have to drive and get lost. And it's got free parking. You know that's going to be a plus since people are paying for the conference. We want to take you to see it today."

Maiya smiled. "Well, that sounds good. But can someone please tell me why we didn't meet there instead today? This way we wouldn't have to drive and get lost. Y'all know how I am. I get lost with the GPS on." She laughed at her own self.

"We did." Angie chuckled.

"What?" Maiya's brows gathered together in confusion.

"*This* is the place we found for the conference," Jasmine explained excitedly.

"Say what now? How? When?" Maiya couldn't contain her excitement either. She fell in love with the building when she drove up today. The beautiful columns, the large parking lot, and the lawn were perfectly maintained. The atmosphere was so peaceful here, just impressive inside and out. Other than that brief encounter with the aloof young man at the desk, she had no bad feelings about the place.

Everybody sighed in relief. They knew how Maiya could be concerning surprises in business, yet they had won her over with this idea.

"Okay, before I get too excited," Maiya said, making herself calm down. "Do we know if they have any of the dates available that we talked about? Have we talked to them about pricing and accommodations? I need some details."

Angie slid a cream-colored folder with gold embossed letters over to her.

Maiya screamed when she opened it. Yes, screamed!

Inside that folder was a contract ready to be signed for the use of the facility. Her team had done all the legwork. They negotiated the pricing for the rooms, which was comparable to the others they forwarded to her. Plus those places didn't have free parking and some were not close to hotels. On top of all that, her team secured three sets of dates, which meant they could decide and get back to the conference center on the final date. They also blocked off several hotel rooms for people who liked conference rates.

Upon realizing that her team was just as committed to this vision as she was, Maiya slid her chair back from the table and went IN! She shouted up something in that meeting room, giving a whole new meaning to the terms 'Victory Room'.

Several people joined her. They were all happy that this idea had been given a green light.

When Maiya finally stopped shouting, she didn't even sit down. "Thank You, Jesus! Let's go, y'all. I want to see everything. Now!"

Everyone moved quickly to take a tour of the building. Thankfully Angie had already cleared the tour with management prior to their arrival.

Leaving the Victory Room, they headed down the hall to the main ballroom where the worship service would take place. As they walked through the lobby again, they passed a restaurant. Seated inside at an intimate table for two was Napoleon. And he was *not* alone!

CHAPTER TEN
Obedience over Instincts

Maiya stopped in her tracks when she spotted Napoleon in the restaurant. He looked like he was engaged in a very intense conversation with the much younger man seated across from him. A bouquet of red roses sat on the table between them.

Maiya's first instinct was to tell her crew to hold up just a minute while she stepped in to talk with her husband. Suddenly she heard the Lord say, *'Don't!'* deep down in her spirit.

Refusing to be disobedient to that direct command, Maiya stayed where she was and just watched Napoleon interact with his companion at the right corner table. The rest of the group must have missed him, because they kept walking down the hallway, thoroughly engrossed in the tour to the point that they hadn't realized that she'd paused for a moment.

Only Angie had noticed her brief tarry. Yet she didn't make anything of it since it appeared as if Maiya was just pausing to look around more closely.

Maiya chose those short lingering moments to try to discern why her husband's companion seemed so familiar. From the side view, he could pass for the young man that she encountered earlier at the front desk. He hadn't held his head up then. He wasn't holding his head up now.

Curiosity scratched at Maiya's mind, but she would not budge until God told her to. *Can I see what's up, Lord?* she prayed, itching to walk up to them and satisfy her curiosity once and for all.

When no green light flashed in her spirit, she reluctantly turned around and headed for the ballroom. It was better to obey the Lord over her instincts. Doing so always put her at an advantage.

Halfway down the hall, Maiya heard someone call her name. She'd know that voice anywhere.

"Maiya, hey baby," Napoleon said from behind her.

She slowly turned around to face him. *I guess You wanted him and a few answers to come to me instead, huh, Lord?*

"Is your meeting over already? I didn't know you would be done so soon. I came to surprise you," Napoleon continued, looking anxious.

Maiya didn't say a word. She just stared at him, noting how rushed his conversation was and how he didn't wait for her to respond to his question before rambling on about something else.

If he really did come to surprise me, why did he leave the roses at the table? He knows how much I love flowers. She raised her right eyebrow at that thought.

"Maiya?" Napoleon prompted, looking concerned now.

"Napoleon, who is that and what are you doing here?" Maiya said, making her first question a double-decker one. Why not get straight to the point? Her voice was calm, but she knew her eyes were flashing fire. She could feel the heat radiating from her pupils.

"I'm waiting." She tapped her feet impatiently, suddenly unwilling to postpone any more of her tour for the sake of somebody else's foolishness.

"Oh, babe, that's just Dwayne Lawson – someone I'm meeting with about a possible minister's fellowship," Napoleon explained. "He's a young preacher and he wants to start a new fellowship, so I'm giving him some advice. Since I was here to surprise you, I thought I'd have my meeting while you had yours. I didn't think you'd be done so soon though."

Maiya kept her face neutral and forced the fire out of her eyes. She saw him intently watching her face for any sign that she might believe him. She refused to show any sign of belief or disbelief until the real truth availed itself.

"I'm not done yet. I have to go view some of the rooms," Maiya replied curtly, ready to end this conversation. "No need for you to wait, because I'll be a while. Love ya. See you later." Then she turned and walked away just as quickly as she'd spoken.

From the reflection of the round mirror in the northeast corner of the hallway, Maiya could see Napoleon looking at her back with a bewildered expression upon his face. He kept glancing from her to the young man still waiting at the table.

"How about a nice dinner out tonight?" he yelled as if needing to get her attention one last time.

"Okay," Maiya replied, refusing to stop or turn around. The farther away she got from Napoleon, the more she felt a significant tugging in her spirit.

'Don't!' she heard the Lord say again. This time she knew that *'Don't'* meant to remain silent, to not say anything...yet.

It was a good thing God put a bridle on Maiya's mouth, because she was known for calling things out quickly. Until He revealed more to her, she would apply prayer to the situation.

God, I don't know the reason for this significant uneasiness I feel in my spirit right now, but I give it to You and pray You reveal it according to Your will. Help me to stay still. Amen, she prayed as she got closer to her destination.

Finally at the ballroom door, Maiya pushed aside any lingering thoughts about her husband before entering the 'Glory Room' as it was aptly called. The rest of the group was already inside. They were walking around and talking about how they could set up the room in various ways. From what she could gather as she approached them, they were torn between banquet and theater style.

"Maiya, what do you think? Banquet style or theater style?" Jasmine asked, soliciting her opinion. "By the way, we know you've been exploring. Why else would it have taken you so long to get in here?"

Almost everyone laughed, having grown used to her exploring ways. Any other day and they would have been totally accurate.

Maiya laughed along with them. Out of the corner of her right eye, she saw Van and Angie engrossed in a sidebar conversation. Nothing unusual there. Along with her, they were usually the masterminds behind the ministry's event planning. Yet it was their body language that gave Maiya pause. Why so tense?

"It's quite lovely," Maiya said, giving Jasmine her full attention now. "You all really did a great job choosing this place. And I absolutely love the names of the rooms. I think theater style would be great for this room."

"It's owned by a Christian family," Jasmine replied. "When we learned that piece of information, we felt that God definitely sent us here."

"Oh that's absolutely wonderful! You all didn't tell me that little tidbit." Maiya smiled again. She knew God brought them here too. It was also God that caused her to look toward the whispering couple in the corner again. "Excuse me, Jas, let me go tear those two apart," she said, referring to Van and Angie who still had their backs turned to everyone.

"Okay, you know they are probably over there making big plans," Jasmine teased.

"You're probably right." Maiya chuckled as she walked away.

Jasmine turned and joined the rest of the group, who now had the answer to their question – theater style on deck!

As Maiya crossed the huge ballroom floor to where Van and Angie were, she suddenly realized that they had seen her husband too. It was as if God had given her super-sonic ears because she heard the tail end of their conversation loud and clear, though it was uttered in whispers.

"Van, I told you that it was him I saw earlier. He had those same roses in his hand. I know he saw me and I swear he was hiding from me. I'm telling Maiya! You know I am," Angie said, crossing her arms.

Van held up his hands. "Hold up, lady. Hold up. Don't go rushing into assumptions. You know how he is. He always likes to surprise her, so maybe that's what the man was trying to do today."

"If that's true, then why didn't he call me?" Angie said, standing akimbo style now. "He always calls me when he's working on a surprise for her. I don't buy it and my spirit tells me something ain't right."

"Well," Van replied, "even if it isn't, you still can't go to Maiya without something concrete. One thing we know about her is that she's very protective of her husband. Besides, if something *is* wrong, she's bound to know it before you tell her."

"You're both right," Maiya said, causing them to jump. They'd been so caught up in their debate that they didn't realize she'd entered the room, much less approached them. "Angie, you're right by saying something is off. I sense it too. I don't know what it is...yet. Van, you're right by saying that we shouldn't jump to conclusions and we're *not* going to do that. What I need both of you to do right now is walk with me back to our group, help us get through this tour and then bring this meeting to a satisfied end. I also need you to make sure I see Allysa once everyone leaves."

Without another word, they turned and made their way back to the middle of the room where the others were. They knew when to challenge her and when not to. This was not a moment to do so.

When they rejoined the rest of the group, Angie immediately took over. "Okay, everyone, let's continue the tour. We need to show Maiya the rooms where we can have breakout sessions if we choose to. Then we're going to head back to the Victory Room. I'm sure all of us have some other things we need to get done today," she said, smoothly making the needed transition back into work mode.

They chatted among themselves as they walked down the hallway. Angie led the way, Maiya followed them out, and Van walked next to her. This was normally how it was. Today was no different. Even so, it was possible that Van discerned how much she needed him right now and thus stayed extra close.

After seeing the six rooms that were available to them, Maiya told everyone to take a fifteen-minute break. They were to meet her back in the Victory Room to talk about the remaining items up for discussion. They'd be done for the day after that.

"I'll be fine," Maiya told Van, who hesitated to leave her side. "You can go on ahead." When he started to protest, she shook her head and firmly said, "Go take a break."

As she walked back towards the meeting room, she knew Napoleon would still be in the building. He never went too far when he suspected that she was angry with him about something. Sure enough he was still in the restaurant when she got back to that area. This time he was alone, drinking coffee and reading a magazine.

"Still here I see," Maiya said, walking up to his table. She kept her face void of emotion.

"Yes, baby. I told you I came to surprise you. I know I said dinner later, but I just thought I'd wait on you anyway." Napoleon stood up to hug and kiss her. He looked surprised when she kissed him back, albeit very briefly.

"Ummm, where are my roses?" Maiya noticed that they were gone now.

"Oh, those were his," Napoleon replied nonchalantly.

"Uh-huh. Well, I've got to go finish up. You don't have to wait. I have another meeting after this one," she informed him. "See you later." Then she kissed his lips again briefly and walked off. Once more Maiya pushed her personal issues to the side and focused on the task at hand as she made her way back to the Victory Room.

Finalizing the conference details went smoothly. Deadlines were set and instructions were given for the next meeting. All they had to do next was finalize the contracts.

Maiya remained seated as everyone exited the room and said their goodbyes. Allysa also remained in the room. Angie had given her instructions not to leave because Maiya needed to have a quick meeting with her.

"Angie said you wanted to see me," Allysa said after Van closed the door on his way out.

"Come closer," Maiya beckoned.

Allysa got up and took the chair next to her. "What's up? If this is about your husband showing up unannounced, you don't have to worry about me saying a word. What happens in your marriage is your business."

I guess she saw him as well. I wonder who else did, Maiya thought, not showing any emotion.

"That's not why I asked to see you," she calmly said. "As for my husband, he was having a meeting, so you can rest easy about that. I asked you to stay, because you and I need to get an understanding right now."

"Oh, really?" Allysa's eyes widened. "About what? Did I do something wrong?"

"Not yet and hopefully after we talk, you won't," Maiya said. "Earlier during our meeting, you voiced some concern about the media and my marriages. Let me assure you, there's nothing to concern yourself with there. Also Angie, Van or I handle all media matters unless it is delegated to someone else. What that means is that if for some reason you are approached by the media, you are to refer them to us. There are no exceptions."

As Maiya spoke, she discerned something new about Allysa – the girl was very status hungry and would do just about anything to get her name recognized. Thus it was imperative that she deal with this matter immediately since she didn't have a red light to shelve it for another time.

"I realize that you are a very talented young lady and could be working anywhere else," Maiya continued. "I appreciate all that you do and I will continue to do my best to make sure that you are all equally recognized for your contributions. This ministry is not about me. It's the work God has called me to, but it takes all of us to bring it to life. You can be sure that your name and work will be just as well-known as anyone else."

Allysa smiled instantly, inadvertently letting Maiya know that she had discerned correctly. "Thank you so much for telling me that. I really do want to do a good job. I've been told that I'm too brass and I should watch what I say and how I say it. I really don't mean to offend anyone," she said, holding her head down.

"Hold your head up, baby girl," Maiya gently encouraged her. "This meeting was not to discourage you, but to assure that we are all a team, all important to this vision and that you'll have your place here as well. You should however consider that wise advice that was given to you. The person who shared that with you obviously cared about you enough to tell you the truth. Go enjoy your day. We'll talk more this week." She gathered up her things and prepared to leave.

"Thanks again and have a good evening." Allysa smiled, standing to her feet.

"Thanks, and you too." Maiya returned her smile.

One down, one to go, she thought to herself as she watched Allysa walk to the door.

CHAPTER ELEVEN
Intertwined Lives

Allysa left the Victory Room and headed straight to the front desk of the conference center. Her legs couldn't move fast enough. She had to talk to Dwayne. He was not only an employee there, but also her new boyfriend. She needed to know what was going on with him and why he hadn't told her that he was meeting with Maiya's husband today.

"Hey you," Allysa said, nearing the desk where he worked.

"Uh...hey. What's up?" Dwayne replied, looking around nervously. "Meeting over?"

"Yes, it is," Allysa said, loving the hazelnut color of his eyes as his gaze finally rested entirely upon her. Right now they looked unsettled, yet she paid that no mind. She was too enamored with the handsome, 6'2 man to focus on minor details like that.

"I have some other things to work on, but..." Allysa chuckled, lowered her voice, and added, "...I can make a little time for you, if you want me to." She smiled, reaching across the counter to touch his left hand. Just that fast she forgot about the inquiries that she wanted to make about his mystery meeting.

"I'd like that a lot." Dwayne grinned sensually as he simultaneously slid the key to Room 309 over to her. "I have a few hours between shifts, so we can spend some time together. I'll meet you there in about thirty minutes. You can take that elevator back there." He nodded towards the service elevator. "No one will see you go up and you don't have to worry about privacy."

Allysa smiled wider and curled her fingers around the key. As she turned away from the desk, she ran right into Maiya. Matter of fact, she almost ran her over. Dwayne's amazing smile and the anticipation of what was about to happen with him soon had her mind gone!

* * * * *

Maiya kept her face neutral after witnessing that whole sordid exchange between Allysa and the man whose nametag read 'Dwayne'. She saw the lust in Dwayne's eyes and the way Allysa's body tensed up when their hands touched. She also saw how quickly the girl's smile dropped when she ran into her.

"Oh, I'm sorry, Maiya. I didn't see you," Allysa said, looking like a deer caught in headlights or at least like a child caught with her hand in the cookie jar.

"Not a problem. I thought you would've sped out of the parking lot by now," Maiya replied, keeping her tone casual. "By the way, do you know that gentleman at the desk?" she probed, concerned for Allysa's emotional well-being. Guilt was an indication that something was wrong somewhere.

Allysa looked back over her shoulder. She tried to hide her smile, but couldn't. "Yes, he's...uh...a friend," she said, returning her attention to Maiya.

"Is he the person that referred us to this place? If so, I'd like to thank him." Maiya headed toward the desk. She would thank Dwayne, yes. But she would also get a good look at him.

"Uh...no, he didn't," Allysa quickly replied, causing her to abruptly stop and turn back around. "Jasmine actually found this place. I didn't know he worked at this location until I told him about the meeting I'd be attending here today."

Silently noting the girl's hasty speech, Maiya easily discerned that Allysa was attempting to hide something. She chose not to press the matter at that moment. "Oh, okay. Well, tell him they have a wonderful facility and I look forward to working with them in the future. I've got to run now. Don't forget what I said."

"Yes, ma'am," Allysa responded in a childlike manner. "I'll definitely tell him."

Maiya walked toward the exit doors. She paused when she got there and looked back just in time to see Allysa head for the service elevator. She shook her head, turned around and left the building.

As Maiya walked to her car, her thoughts turned from Allysa and Dwayne to Napoleon. She knew something was amiss, but she just wasn't sure what it was yet. Resisting the urge to jump to conclusions, she decided to take a few hours and clear her mind. That was the best thing for her to do since she had a doctor's appointment later today and didn't need any additional stress before going. Afterwards she'd talk to her husband.

Sliding into her car against the smooth leather, Maiya took a deep breath and blew it out. As the breath slowly exited her body, she noticed a ball of tension in her shoulders. That was enough to provoke a spontaneous

48

decision – Massage Point would be her next stop. A few hours of pampering, some smooth jazz and she'd be ready to move on with the rest of this day.

Picking up her phone, Maiya called ahead to make sure her favorite massage therapist, Cameron, was on duty today. Cameron was a young man that she inadvertently started mentoring when she first visited Massage Point. After suffering with bouts of depression, anxiety, and anger as a result of his childhood abandonment and abuse, he'd made a lot of progress in his life. God orchestrated their paths to cross and she was happy to have met him.

"Hi, this is Maiya Jackson. I'm calling to see if Cameron is in today and if he has any available slots soon," she said to the young lady that answered the phone.

"Yes, ma'am. He's in today," the pleasant female replied. "He has a client now, but is scheduled to be done in about ten minutes. I can schedule you for the next opening if you'd like."

"Yes, thank you so much! I'll be there in about thirty minutes," Maiya said.

Hanging up the phone, she sighed and then turned on her favorite Rachelle Ferrell CD. The music and the lyrics were equally relaxing to her. The tension in her shoulders gradually started to subside.

Realizing that she needed more than a CD could give her right now, Maiya turned the music off and prayed. "Lord, I know that You already know what the source of this tension is. I pray You reveal it to me and show me how to deal with it wisely. Help me not to jump to conclusions. But I'll be honest, something is not right and I do not want to go through another fiasco like before with Napoleon. Show me what I need to know and what I need to do. In Jesus Name, Amen." She drove the remaining distance in silence listening for the voice of the Lord.

When she arrived at Massage Point, Cameron greeted her at the door. The twenty-three-year-old young man was quiet, so well-mannered and always nicely groomed.

"Hi there, pretty lady," Cameron said, ushering her inside.

"Hello there, young man. You're smiling today!" She was happy to see the smile actually reaching up and into his eyes today. That hadn't always been the case before. "How are you?"

"I'm really great. I have something to tell you," he said, leading her to the room that he prepared for her.

"Oh really, what's that now?" Maiya asked excitedly, hoping it was good news. She waved to the young lady that worked at the receptionist station as she passed by.

"I'll let you get changed first, then we can talk during our session," Cameron said, courteously holding the door open for her.

They affectionately called Maiya's massage times 'our session' because that's when he usually opened up to her and shared details of his life. She also prayed and poured into him during those times.

"Okay, one minute and I'll be ready," Maiya said as he closed the door. She dropped her purse in the green and blue corner chair nearby and then took off her shoes. She quickly undressed, draped a white sheet about her body, and then stored her clothing in the empty blue cubicle below the linen shelf.

"Knock, Knock," Cameron said, returning to the door about two minutes later.

"Come on in." Maiya opened the door, ready to hear what he had to share. "Well, don't keep me waiting. What's going on in your world?" she said once she was seated on the long padded table.

"All right, all right." Cameron warmed the lilac scented lotion in his hands by rubbing them together. "Lay down and I'll tell you, Mama," he said, calling her by the nickname he'd given her about a year ago after their third conversation.

"I'm listening." Smiling, Maiya closed her eyes as she reclined on her stomach. She was pretty fond of that nickname and honored that he'd chosen it considering he never really had a mother. As a foster child, he was bounced around to different homes until he aged out of the system at eighteen.

"Well, you know we've been talking about me going to church and actually being active. So this past Thursday, I went to a service and I felt so different at this church," he said, massaging the lotion into her stiff shoulders. "I felt like I do when we talk. I felt like God was hearing me and that I could hear God."

"That is so awesome," Maiya replied, her eyes still closed as his competent hands melted away the tension in her shoulders. "I'm so happy you haven't given up on finding a church home. I want you to be in a place that will help you grow."

"Well, that's not all," Cameron said excitedly. "I joined. I'm going to start the new member orientation next week. After that, I will start my regular study classes and I'm looking into working with some of the different ministries there. They have so many to choose from, but the two I want to work with most are the homeless and orphans group." He continued to work the tension out of Maiya's back as he rambled happily about his new church home.

Silent tears flowed from her eyes. They had talked about this many times and prayed together. Now God had finally manifested the answer to those prayers. The fact that Cameron had joined a church meant that God was healing those old wounds and closing his heart to distrust. More good news was just what the doctor ordered.

50

"What's the name of the church? Who is the Pastor?" Maiya asked, sharing his excitement and wanting to know more about the church her 'son' would be attending.

"Divine Grace Ministries in the Stone Mountain area. The Pastor is Apostle Benjamin Martin."

Maiya opened her eyes, looked back at him and smiled.

"I told him about you. He said he knows you very well. That confirmed to me even more that I was in the right place." He smiled and started working on her arms.

"Yes, I know Apostle Martin very well," she said, facing forward again as her eyes dried. "Actually, I served with him for many years. He's a great Pastor. I'm really glad to know you're connected there. What a small world. You have to keep me posted now. I'm still here when you need me." Maiya meant every word she said. Though she was happy he had a Pastor now, she wanted him to know that she was still available to help any way she could.

"Oh yes, ma'am. I definitely will and thanks." His hands moved upward to massage her scalp.

Maiya moaned. Scalp massages were heavenly to her. Closing her eyes again, she silently thanked God for how He was moving in Cameron's life and carrying the young man forward in a positive direction.

When the massage was over, Cameron thanked Maiya again for all of her help and support. Then he left the room so she could re-dress. "I'll be waiting just outside the door," he said on his way out.

Two minutes was all it took for her to get dressed. "Ok, I'm ready," Maiya announced, coming out of the massage room with extra pep in her step. Her shoulders weren't tight anymore and her soul was encouraged by his good news. "I feel so much better."

"Glad to hear that. And by the way, your massage is on the house today, Mama," Cameron said, surprising her with even more good news. "I just wanted to give you a gift for all you've done for me. I know they may have just been random conversations to you, but I have really changed because of them. I'm not the same. This change began when I met and started talking to you. So thank you. Thank you very much." He leaned down and gave her a peck on the cheek.

"Well, thank you, son! I'm thankful God allowed our paths to cross, but I'm not going anywhere. Just because you have a church home now doesn't mean I'm going to drop out of your life," Maiya said, reiterating what she said earlier. "As a matter of fact, here is my home number. So whenever you want to call, you can," she added with a wide smile, giving him a business card with her personal number on the back. God had given her another son. She intended to fully embrace him.

Tears sprang to Cameron's eyes as he received the card like it was a precious stone. "Ma, are you for real?" He jumped when he asked that question.

"Yes, son, I'm for real. Mama loves you. Now you better get back to work, because my children have to work," Maiya said, halfway laughing.

"Yes, ma'am." Cameron laughed, too, as they walked to the front parlor together. Today he walked her all the way out to her car. Both wore big cheddar-cheese grins upon their face, causing the people around them to smile as well.

After they said their goodbyes at the car, Cameron went back to the building to prepare for his next client. Maiya headed to her final appointment of the day.

As she pulled out of the parking lot, her phone rang. It was Napoleon. She immediately clicked the answer button on the steering wheel.

"Hi there," she said.

"Hi, beautiful," he answered. "Are we still on for tonight?"

"Yes, but how about dinner in rather than out?" she half-asked and half-told him.

"Well, okay." Napoleon suddenly sounded distracted. "Baby, let me get to this next meeting and I'll see you tonight. I love you so much. Bye," he said in a rush.

"I love you too. See you later," she said, starkly aware of his hasty tone before the call ended.

* * * * *

Napoleon's attention snapped from his cell phone to the door as someone entered the room he occupied. It was Allysa.

"Well, well, look who actually showed up," he said, perusing her frame from head to toe.

"What are *you* doing here?" Allysa asked defensively, closing the door behind her. "I'm supposed to be meeting Dwayne here in a few minutes."

"I guess that makes two of us then." Napoleon laughed. It was apparent that she didn't have a clue what was going on.

"Why would he be meeting you here? I thought you all finished your meeting earlier. I want to know what's going on and I'm not leaving until I do," Allysa said, slinging her purse upon the Victorian style chair near the door and then kicking off her shoes.

"Yeah, we were just about finished. Have a seat. Would you like a drink?" Napoleon offered, pointing to the well-stocked enclosed bar.

"Ah, no thanks." She sat in the chair beside her purse. "I'll just wait for Dwayne. How do you know him anyway?"

"We are partnering together on a new ministry venture. We're just good friends." Napoleon got up and poured himself a glass of Crown Royal. He saw her watching his every move with curiosity in her eyes. No doubt she had taken in the fact that his shirt and shoes were off, leaving him dressed only in a t-shirt and trousers. He hoped she liked what she saw. He sure liked what he saw.

"So what's your story with Dwayne?" Napoleon wanted to satisfy his own curiosity.

"We just started dating. I guess you can call it that," Allysa said hesitantly.

"I guess you can call it that," Napoleon repeated, committing that statement to memory. "That's interesting. *We* should be friends, you know. You are working with Prophetess now, so I'm sure we'll be seeing a great deal of each other."

Allysa frowned. "What is *really* going on here?" She turned just in time to see Dwayne walking in the door. "Maybe *you're* the best person to ask. What is really going on here, Dwayne?" she said, redirecting her question to him.

Dwayne looked from her to Napoleon without saying a word. Then he closed the door, locked it, and walked fully into the room. "I'm off for the rest of the day," he said, speaking to no one in particular.

"Looks like we have more time then." Napoleon spoke to Dwayne, but kept his eyes on Allysa.

"Excuse me, more time for what?" She stood up and turned to face Dwayne completely. "What is he talking about? I came up here to be with *you.*" Her eyes narrowed. Her face registered confusion.

In response, Dwayne wrapped his arms around her and kissed her squarely on the mouth. Though caught off guard, Allysa melted into his kiss. While he kissed her, he kept his eyes open to watch Napoleon who stood behind them.

Napoleon smiled and winked at Dwayne. *This little deal just might work out,* he thought, greedily licking his lips.

Putting his glass down, Napoleon walked over to them. He grabbed Allysa from behind, swung her around and then kissed her more passionately than Dwayne had. She never saw it coming, didn't stand a chance of stopping it. When she finally realized what was going on, he felt her wrestle against him trying to pull away.

The harder Allysa fought, the tighter Napoleon held her. He snatched her small frame up and molded her closer to his body. Knowing the right places to put his hands, he remained consistent with his sensual caresses until she finally surrendered to his kiss.

Meanwhile, Dwayne watched in shock, silence, and smoldering jealousy.

CHAPTER TWELVE
You Said What?

Turning into the parking lot of her doctor's office, Maiya felt strong and ready to have her annual exam. She felt peace after she prayed and allowed God to minister to her on the drive there. Although she knew something still wasn't quite right, she stood firm in her trust that the Lord would work it out. Ever since she stepped out on faith and started the ministry, pursuing the things God had spoken to her, she learned more and more to trust Him with everything, especially herself.

Maiya parked her car in the nearly empty lot, grabbed her purse and exited the vehicle. She wore a smile on her face, because after she heard God say, *'It will work out for your good'*, that's the report she chose to believe.

The first person she saw when she entered the building was Carol Perkins, the kind-hearted woman that worked at the front desk. Carol just rededicated her life to Christ a few months ago at the young age of fifty-nine. She'd been smiling ever since.

"Good afternoon, Mrs. Jackson," Carol said with a wide smile.

"Hi there, Miss Carol. How are you?" Maiya replied. "You look absolutely wonderful as usual."

"Oh praise the Lord. It's all because of Him." Carol pointed her right index finger upward. "You know I almost died a few months ago, but God spared my life, so I *feel* wonderful too."

"Hallelujah!" Maiya clapped her hands. "Our God is good!"

"Yes, He is." Carol chuckled. "Dr. Washington is ready to see you. You can go on back, so you can get out of here and live!" Her smile never faded. Nor the excitement from her voice.

"Thank you. What room am I going to today?" Maiya asked.

"Angel knows. She's waiting for you right inside the door. She'll get you settled into your designated room," Carol replied.

"Yes, ma'am. It was good to see you today." Maiya waved goodbye as she walked through the door toward the examination area. "Hi, Angel," she said, greeting the woman that stood waiting for her.

"Hello there. Are you ready to get started today?" Angel asked.

"Yes, as ready as I can be," Maiya said.

"Well let's get your weight and vitals, then I'll take you to exam room three." Angel led her to the first room on the left.

Maiya silently thanked God when she learned that her blood pressure was great and that she'd lost a few pounds. She'd been losing weight and didn't even realize it. Her iron level was up to eleven. That was an improvement from the last visit. She'd get more in-depth information once she talked to the doctor, whom she'd been seeing for the past twelve years.

After being led to exam room three, Maiya waited for Dr. Laila Washington to come perform the Pap smear and breast exam. She hated this yearly exam, but deemed it a necessary part of being a woman. Angel had made sure all of the essential instruments and supplies were prepped on a nearby wheeled table.

Not quite a minute later, there was a knock on the door. "Come in," Maiya said. "Hi there, lady. How are you?" she continued when her doctor entered the room.

"I'm good, stranger." Dr. Washington smiled. "I don't think I've seen you in here in a year," she teased, knowing full well that Maiya only came to see her when absolutely necessary. "How have you been?" She went over to the sink and washed her hands.

"I've been great."

"That's good. I've been following the ministry and it looks like you're progressing. Is it true that there is a conference coming up soon?" Dr. Washington asked, putting on latex gloves as she prepared for the exam. She normally talked to her patients while examining them to make them comfortable during the process and to take their focus off the exam. It worked for Maiya every time.

"Yes, there is another conference coming up and you know I want you to be there." Maiya knew the process by now, so she laid back and closed her eyes. "That last presentation you did for us during the day conference we had was phenomenal. I believe it was life changing for some of the women."

"I wouldn't miss it for the world," Dr. Washington said excitedly, performing her duties with adroit hands. "I love your ministry beyond walls concept. The fact that you recognize we must minister to the whole person including health, wealth and spiritual needs is awesome. Please make sure I get the dates because I'm definitely going to be there. I haven't heard you preach in..." She paused in deep thought. "...in too long," she finished after that long pause.

They laughed together. Even though they were doctor and patient, they'd also formed a friendship.

"Alrighty, ma'am. I'm done," Dr. Washington said, putting her instruments aside. "That wasn't too bad now, was it?"

"That's why I keep coming to you. I barely felt a thing and you know how I feel about those pelvic exams." Maiya laughed as she sat up.

"You do have some discharge located deep in your vaginal area that I'm going to check out. It could just be yeast or bacteria, but I want to be sure it's nothing abnormal," Dr. Washington informed as she peeled off her gloves and discarded them in a nearby waste basket.

"Okay. I haven't had a bacterial infection since I had the hysterectomy in '07," Maiya said.

"Sit tight, I'll be back in a few minutes," Dr. Washington replied, washing her hands again.

"Can I get dressed?" Maiya asked as the doctor headed for the door with the tray of cultures.

"Yes, ma'am, we are all done. I'm going to test these cultures myself for added privacy," Dr. Washington replied.

"I appreciate that." Maiya nodded her gratitude.

"You're welcome. I just want to make sure I'm treating you properly." Dr. Washington smiled and then left the room.

I wasn't expecting anything to be abnormal, but I'm sure it's nothing serious, Maiya thought, mulling over what she'd been told as she put on her clothes.

While she waited, she looked through a magazine on the counter next to her. She stopped at an article about living in the overflow. The content of the article was about overflow being more than simply tangible items, but also a mindset. She looked toward the bottom of the page, searching for the contributor of the article or a website for more information.

When Maiya looked up, it was twenty minutes later according to the wooden clock on the wall. *Wow! Didn't realize I'd been reading for that long,* she thought just as the door opened.

"What is it?" Maiya instantly noticed the blank look on Dr. Washington's face.

"Maiya, I don't really know how to tell you this. I ran this test several times before I came back in here with this news." Dr. Washington looked down at the paper while shaking her head. "*Several* times just to be *absolutely* sure."

Maiya sprung to her feet. "Laila, what is it?" She addressed her informally as they often did when they were talking one-on-one.

"Sit down," Dr. Washington said, taking the seat across from her. "You have an STD. It's called—"

"A what?!" Maiya interrupted, feeling her eyes stretch in their sockets as she returned to her seat. "Girl, I know you didn't just tell me I have a sexually transmitted disease. What did you say?" She bent her head slightly to the right, trying to make sure she'd heard correctly in her shock.

"That's what I said when I ran this for the fourth time. That's what took me so long. I had to be absolutely sure. Let me first tell you, it's curable. So thank God for that, but you definitely have an STD. It's called Trichomoniasis."

"I don't understand. I don't have any symptoms and I haven't had any discharge or odor. Why didn't I know something was wrong? You said its curable, right?" Maiya asked, deeply disturbed by this news. Her mind wasn't quite racing, but she was more than ready to get home now. As her only partner, Napoleon had some explaining to do.

"Yes, thank God. It is curable. I've already written your antibiotic prescription. After a few days, it will be cleared up. As for why you didn't know, this particular disease can lie dormant in you for weeks, months, even years without symptoms showing up. However, it can be detected when the proper tests are done. Most people don't know until they go to the doctor. Many times they aren't there for that reason, but they find out just as you did today."

Maiya listened intently while her mind turned, trying to make sense of all this. She had the same exam done last year, but everything was normal. Why was that?

"Let me ask you a question. Could this have been there at my last visit and we simply missed it?" Maiya needed her to say yes.

"No. After you confided in me the reasons you were requesting specific tests last year, I ran all of them including this one. If it was there, I would have found it," Dr. Washington replied, watching her closely, as if looking for a reaction. There was none.

Maiya honestly didn't know how to feel. She didn't really know what to say, so she remained quiet. She dropped her head and listened even more intently.

"Maiya, I'm sorry," Dr. Washington said in a comforting tone. "I know the ordeal you've been through before and the months we spent testing you to make sure all was well. But as I said, this is curable, so even though it's not what you would want to hear, don't forget to thank God for what He's done even in this."

"I see. Was there anything else?" Maiya asked.

"No, everything else is fine. You're going to be just fine physically. Before I let you leave, do you want to talk about what you're feeling?" Dr. Washington spoke as her friend now rather than her physician.

"Right now I feel numb, but I'm not going into shut down so don't worry about that." Maiya stood to her feet. "I'm about to go home and deal with this. Thank you for your concern and for protecting me. I'll be in touch soon." She picked up her purse and headed out the door. Halfway there, she turned and asked, "Can you put today's charges on my credit card that you have on file? I don't want to have to stop at the desk on my way out."

"I'll take care of it. All is well. Go take care of you," Dr. Washington assured her.

Maiya nodded and then turned to leave. Her mind was in overdrive as she walked down the hallway towards the front exit. When she left the building, a silent breeze graced her, causing her to stop in her tracks.

For a brief moment, Maiya stood still in the breeze, not saying anything, not thinking. She just stood still. When the breeze seemed to settle, she headed to her car.

She drove in silence for a good fifteen minutes. When the lyrics of her most recently released single bubbled up in her spirit, she started singing them. "You are my hiding place. My strength when I am weak. My joy when I'm sad. My laughter when I'm mad. You are my hiding place."

You Are My Hiding Place calmed Maiya down to the point where she could finally make her next move. She picked up her cell phone and called her husband.

Napoleon didn't answer. Three phone calls later and he still didn't answer.

Maiya decided against leaving a message, so she just hung up. Then she headed home.

Lord, I only ask You for two things – wisdom and help controlling my temper, she prayed.

'It will work out for your good', she heard God reiterate from earlier today.

Maiya nodded in full acceptance of that Rhema word. It was enough for her to rest in. It had to be.

CHAPTER THIRTEEN
Double-Crossed

Maiya's cell phone rang just as she pulled into the garage. It was her ministry line. She let it ring a few times, contemplating about whether or not she should answer it.

Remembering that the ringing of that particular line meant someone was in need, perhaps even more than her right now, prompted Maiya to finally answer the call. "This is Prophetess Maiya, how may I help you?" She tried to add some life to her voice that she wasn't feeling at the moment.

"Hi, Prophetess. This is Minister Charlene. I know you said you would have your assistant to call, but I wanted to call you back and tell you thank you again," she said, speaking quickly.

"You are quite welcome. How was the rest of your day?" Maiya asked, discerning that she needed to talk more.

"It has been a rough day," Charlene began. "I didn't go to work. I stayed home to put him out. We fought and he hit me again, so I called the police, but not until after I stabbed him. I couldn't beat him, but I wasn't going to let him kill me. The truth is, I was so enraged when he hit me again that I wanted to murder him in cold blood until I remembered your words from this morning. I was about to negatively alter my entire life because of someone else and I couldn't do that. I know it was God that we talked before this happened again," she said, not even stopping to take a breath. "I may still need your help. For now I wanted you to know I'm out of that. I'm not going back. I've just got to find a way to move forward."

"It sounds like you had a pretty eventful day. I must say I'm glad you didn't kill him and that God had already intervened. You sound firm on your decision not to go back to him, so I pray that the peace of God is with you during your transition. It may not be easy but it will be worth it," Maiya shared. "I've been in an abusive relationship before and getting out seemed harder than staying, but saving my life was worth it. God didn't create us to be anyone's punching bag."

"Right. Well, I don't want to hold you, but I just felt like I needed to tell you what happened today. I look forward to our next conversation," Charlene said, sounding very resolved.

"We'll speak again soon. Be blessed!" Maiya said. As the call ended, she was grateful that she answered the phone. It took her mind off of her current situation and she heard God through Charlene's words.

Don't alter your life negatively because of someone else.

Maiya remained in the car, meditating on those words a little while longer. When she was done, she went into the house to face Napoleon. He was already home based on the presence of his car in the garage.

As she walked into the family room, she heard his phone ringing. At first she didn't pay any attention to it. His phone rang all the time. Both of their phones did, so that was not unusual.

However Maiya felt compelled to answer Napoleon's phone today. Blame it on the different ringtone and the constant back-to-back ringing, followed by repeated text messages dinging. They all annoyed her, prompting her to answer his phone just to put an end to the noise.

Napoleon's phone stopped ringing just as she made it to the counter where it lay face down. Leaving it where it was, Maiya walked back into the family room and sat down in her favorite chair. She knew he'd be downstairs at some point to answer his phone. She decided to just wait until he surfaced.

While she waited, she mentally prepared herself for their imminent conversation. Inside she was borderline raging, yet she was determined to let God lead her even in this situation.

After about ten minutes, true to form, Napoleon came downstairs and headed straight for his phone, wearing different clothes than he had on this morning. He didn't bother to look around. Otherwise he would have seen her.

"We need to talk," Maiya said, startling him. Her words were simple, but her tone was potent. They instantly got his attention.

"H...hey, baby. I didn't hear you come in. I was upstairs in the shower. Was my phone ringing? I thought I heard it," Napoleon said, quickly recovering from his shock as he walked toward the chair she sat in.

"Let me ask you something, Napoleon. And you only have ONE chance to tell me the truth." Maiya pierced him with her eyes as she spoke.

"Baby, what is it?" He sounded genuinely concerned.

"When did you know you had an STD?" she asked bluntly.

Surprise registered all over his face. He stopped short in his tracks. His body language indicated that he was caught, yet he refused to admit it.

"A what? I don't have an STD," Napoleon refuted, trying to look and sound innocent.

"Maybe not now, but you had one and now *I* have one." Maiya felt her anger rising quickly at the nerve of this man. Liar!

"Maiya, what are you talking about?" He turned and walked toward his phone, which was now on its third ring.

"Cut the bull!" Maiya shouted, springing to her feet. "I just left the doctor's office and I have an STD." She got up in his face. "And let's be very clear about this, YOU are my only bed partner." She pointed accusingly at him.

Napoleon remained quiet. Instead he quickly silenced his phone and put it in his lower right pocket.

Maiya took a deep breath and rephrased her words, despite her increasing anger. "Okay, I'm going to try this a different way. When did you start back cheating?"

"I'm not cheating!" he swore, raising both hands above his head.

"Then how do you explain me having an STD? I told you the last time we went through this bull that I was not, absolutely *not* putting up with this foolishness again. I guess you didn't believe me." She turned and walked away from him. It was either walk away or knock the hell out of him!

"Where are you going?" he demanded to know as she walked toward the staircase.

Maiya didn't answer him. She just shook her head, not believing that it had come to this all over again. Lies and now an STD.

So much for those days being over, she thought, feeling betrayed all over again.

* * * * *

Napoleon was about to pursue Maiya when his phone started buzzing in his pocket. He yanked it out and saw that it was Dwayne calling again. He waited until his wife was upstairs before answering.

"Hello," Napoleon said in a hushed, irritated tone. "Why are you calling me back to back?"

"I want to know what that was about today in the hotel room?" Dwayne ranted. "The deal was you could watch *me* with her, not the other way around. You said you wanted to talk to her about your wife. What was all that other stuff?"

"I got so excited watching you kiss her that I wanted to kiss her for myself. I wanted to see what you liked about her so much. You didn't seem so broken up about me calling *us* off, so I wanted to know what the little tramp had," Napoleon snapped back. "What's the big deal anyway? She couldn't be *that* into you if she let me get that so quickly." He laughed.

"Man, you are married, remember? You're the one who said you were out of this *because* of your marriage, so whatever. That bull you pulled today is not cool. I bet you wouldn't think it was so funny if your precious wife knew what you'd really been up to, Mr. I'm-Running-Revivals," Dwayne said, sounding full of hurt and rage.

"Hold on," Napoleon told him as another call beeped in. He looked at the panel and smiled. It was Allysa. "Talk to big daddy," he said, immediately answering her call.

"This is Allysa. I'm not going to meet you tomorrow. I've already crossed the line once and I'm not going to do that to Maiya again. I'm not going to say anything to her, but count me out," she said hastily.

"It's not like she's ever going to know. I've been doing Dwayne for years and she has never suspected a thing. Come on now, you know you liked how I put this whip on you, girl," he said cockily. "We could have a love triangle."

Allysa made a gagging sound at those words. "I thought something was suspicious between y'all earlier today, but I had no idea you were lovers. So hell no!" she said firmly. "Do whatever you want, but I'm not going to be a part of it. I got caught up today. I can't believe I actually slept with you. Maiya's my boss and she's been so good to me. You should be ashamed of yourself, but then so should I. Don't call me again. And to make sure you don't, I'm changing my number. Tonight!" Then she hung up without another word.

Napoleon shrugged and clicked back over to Dwayne, who was still holding on the other line. "Listen, I decided I'm not going to fool around with that girl anymore. She's probably too much drama and I don't need that. It took me years to get Maiya to trust me again, so why mess up this money train I got going?" he said arrogantly.

"Are you serious?" Dwayne replied. "You were just ready to use Allysa to spy on your wife's upcoming plans just to make sure she wasn't keeping anything from you. In fact, you were *too* ready to destroy Maiya because no one is calling you and yet they are chasing *her* down for speaking *and* singing engagements. I can't even believe you just said that. You're a sick, jealous bastard. I don't know why I even love you," Dwayne said, sounding as if he was questioning his own judgment.

"You love what I do for you and what I do *to* you. I'll be over in an hour," Napoleon said and abruptly ended the call before Dwayne could protest.

Before today, Dwayne might have not protested even if Napoleon had stayed on the phone. He never protested before. Not in all the tumultuous years they'd been together. Things changed after Allysa came on the scene. Even more so now that Napoleon had slept with her.

Shrugging off that whole encounter, Napoleon went upstairs to the master suite. The door was locked. He didn't bother to knock or say anything to Maiya. He simply went down the back stairs and exited the house. He'd deal with his wife later. He had some making up to do with Dwayne right now.

* * * * *

Maiya waited upstairs until she heard Napoleon's car pull out of the garage. She hadn't heard everything he said to the person on the phone, but she heard enough to know he was cheating…again!

Now that the coast was clear, Maiya walked downstairs and retrieved her phone from her purse. She called the first person that dropped in her spirit. "Hey, Van. Do you have a minute? I need to talk to you," she said as soon as he answered.

"Hey, and yes, I do. Let me close this door," Van replied.

"Okay." Maiya heard him tell Janine who was calling and that he'd be right back. All signs of a virtuous man!

"What's wrong? I hear it in your voice and I don't like it," Van said when he returned to the phone. "My spirit is picking up all kinds of things on the radar," he added, referring to his gift of discernment.

"Listen to me, I need you praying and I need you and Angie to continue handling the conference plans without me for a while," Maiya said. "I have something urgent I need to deal with and I don't know how it's going to play out right now. What I'm about to tell you I know will stay between us, so listen real good, okay?"

"Maiya, what has happened since earlier today? We had a great meeting besides the little episode with Allysa. What's wrong?" Van asked, repeating his earlier question.

"It's Napoleon. He's cheating again," she said, not bothering to fix it up or try to cover it up. There was no need to. This was Van she was talking to.

"What!" was his first response. "Maiya, are you sure? You two have been so happy and things have been going so great. Are you *absolutely* sure?"

"Yes, and the STD that I have proves it." Though thoroughly embarrassed to reveal something so personal, she knew that it was necessary to give him the raw truth.

"What do you want me to do? You name it and it's done," Van said, sounding angry and yet being helpful at the same time.

"Right now, I need you to make sure everything we've worked so hard for stays intact. I'll call you later. Love you. And thank you," Maiya said. Her eyes filled with tears, but she refused to let them fall.

"Love you too, My," Van said, calling her by his own special nickname. A nickname that he only used for special occasions. "I'm so sorry. I'm here when you need me. Anytime."

"Although I know you won't tell anyone, I want you to tell Angie and Star. I simply don't have the strength to repeat it. Not tonight, so please do me that favor," Maiya said, starting to feel drained from this conversation.

"I will."

"Thanks again. And by the way, I'm turning my phone off for the rest of the night, so tell her don't worry," Maiya said and then promptly ended the call.

It was time to go back to her secret place and stay awhile.

CHAPTER FOURTEEN
And There's More

Early the next morning, Napoleon called Maiya's phone several times. Nine times to be exact. Each time it went straight to voicemail. He was not surprised considering the fact that he'd given her an STD and didn't come home last night. Nevertheless, he got in his car and sped to their house.

Maiya's anger had actually worked in Napoleon's favor. It gave him a convenient excuse to stay out late in order to let her cool off. It also gave him an opportunity to quiet the rantings of Dwayne and Cierra. The latter was yet another longtime lover of his.

Napoleon visited Dwayne first. A few charming words, smiles, sensual touches, and more empty promises were all it took to calm him down. He lied to Dwayne again by telling him that he was going straight home as usual.

Napoleon went to see Cierra instead. It took a little bit more to pacify her, even though she was simple-minded and usually believed anything he said. Cierra was peeved with him for not spending as much time with her anymore. In order to calm her down, he decided to spend the night at her home, thereby proving his love for her...so she thought.

Now all he needed to do was get through to Maiya. Then things would be back to *his* version of normal. At the thought of his wife, Napoleon called her again. This time it rang three times before going to voicemail.

"So she finally turned her phone back on," he said aloud, not appreciating the fact that she deliberately didn't answer his call. Turning the phone off to avoid answering everybody's call was understandable. Deliberately not answering *his* call was unacceptable!

* * * * *

He has some nerve trying to call me after being out all night! Maiya thought, sending Napoleon's latest call to voicemail as well. She knew he hadn't come home last night because she was up for most of the night herself. In fact, she'd only had an hour of sleep.

Forcing her legs to get out of bed, Maiya headed for the shower. She needed to get to the pharmacy and pick up her two prescriptions. Though she was still in shock that she had an STD of all things, there was no need to delay her healing process.

"Lord, I really feel like cussing right now! This…" Maiya stopped before she actually spoke her thoughts out loud. It was bad enough that those words were already running fluently through her head. "Lord Jesus, help me," she said, turning on the shower.

With her mind wandering, Maiya stood under the gentle spray and let the water wash her tears away. Those tears flowed from behind the barriers she'd been building all night.

Leaning against the shower wall, she cried out to God from the depths of her sorrow. "Lord, I really didn't want to fail this time. I've tried so hard to work on this marriage and not give up. But God, I really can't take any more. An STD, really?" More tears flowed.

When Maiya was composed enough, she finished her shower, got dressed and pulled her hair up into a ponytail. She didn't want anything touching her neck, creating unnecessary irritation at a time when she was irritated enough.

Suddenly she heard the garage open. Not ready to see Napoleon yet, Maiya hastily grabbed her phone and purse, and then headed down the back stairs. Once she heard him enter the house, she slipped out and left.

Thank God I'm already dressed, she thought, quickly starting her car.

She also thanked God that Napoleon had left the garage door open. It made it that much easier to back out before he could stop her. And he did try to stop her once he heard her car start.

Maiya didn't even bother to look at him. She just kept backing up until she was clear to speed away. A few seconds later, her phone went off. It was a text message. She didn't bother to look at that either. She already knew who it was – Napoleon.

Go take a shower and remove the evidence like you always do, Maiya thought, recalling him taking a shower immediately after coming home too many times to count. He didn't work in construction or lawn care, so why the constant urgency about getting clean the second he walked into the house?

After picking up her medicine, Maiya went back home. Strangely, it didn't feel like home anymore. Would it ever feel that way again? Although she'd rather be anywhere but here, her eyes were so puffy and red that she knew she would draw unwanted attention to herself if she was out in public.

Times like this, I wish I'd chosen to have an office away from home, Maiya thought. She could have gone to Angie, Van, or Star's house, but she didn't want to put them in the middle of this. She knew Napoleon would go to their homes if she didn't come back. Besides that, she knew that she had to confront this issue head-on and the sooner, the better. She learned from past experiences that running or ignoring the issue would not make it go away.

As predicted, Napoleon was taking a shower when she entered the house. She heard his phone ringing again from upstairs. Her irritation level rose even higher. Who was calling him now? And why?

Yes, the back to back ringing annoyed her, but it was the ringtone that aggravated her the most. Hearing *There Goes My Baby* by Charlie Wilson was *her* ringtone. It was the one Napoleon assigned to her incoming calls. She wasn't calling him, so why was that song playing on his phone?

Let me make sure. Maiya quickly checked her phone to be certain she wasn't accidentally calling him via pocket dial. She did have her purse held tightly against her, possibly causing the phone inside to start dialing someone.

Nope. It's not me, Maiya surmised after checking her phone log. Besides, that ringtone was still playing, so there was no way it could be her calling him.

Suddenly Napoleon's phone stopped ringing. Just as suddenly he appeared at the bottom of the stairs. He wore a purple satin robe that reached all the way down to his calves. In the upper right corner were his overlapping initials in white. She'd personally ordered that monogrammed robe for him as a birthday gift.

"Why are you calling me and we're in the same house?" Napoleon asked in a casual tone, as if he was asking why the sky was blue. The shifting of his eyes betrayed him. So did that tight grip he had on his phone.

That was enough to make Maiya snap. "You know damn well that was not me calling you! Don't even start that bull today! I don't want to hear it!" She couldn't believe he was standing there trying to look innocent, like he hadn't assigned some other woman the same ringtone.

"Cursing is not becoming of a Prophetess," he reprimanded.

"And being a hoe ain't cute for a Bishop," Maiya retorted. She reached deeper into her purse and snatched out the two prescription bottles. "Napoleon, do you know what these are?" She held the bottles high in the air. "They are the antibiotics I have to take because of the STD *you* gave me. Now we can take all day to do this or you can just tell the truth."

"I already told you that I don't have an STD and I haven't had one. Maybe there is something *you* want to tell me," he said, throwing the shade of suspicion her way.

This lying ni— She quickly arrested her thoughts. *Nope. I'm not going there. That's the old Maiya.*

"Nice try, but knowing you, you probably went to the doctor months ago and got treated," she said aloud.

"Listen, baby, let's sit down and talk," Napoleon petitioned in a gentler tone. "Whatever you think is going on, I promise you it's not. I told you after that last mess up that those days were over. Baby, you're all I need. I'd be a fool to be with anyone but you." He reached for her.

Maiya slapped his hand away. "What you're not going to do is put your filthy hands on me. Don't act like you've forgotten who I am. This ain't what you want," she said, not-so-subtly reminding him of her past. She'd been known to fight a man before and would fight one again if she ever had to.

Before Napoleon could say anything, his phone started playing *There Goes My Baby* again. He quickly silenced it. "I must have assigned the wrong caller to that song. Let me fix that right now, because that's your song, baby, and no one else's," he explained, studying her face as if searching for a reaction. He didn't get one.

Refusing to give him anything else he didn't deserve, Maiya turned her back on him and went over to her favorite chair. She sat down, and pulled her purple and gold blanket over her head. She closed her eyes and started to pray.

* * * * *

Keeping an eye on Maiya, Napoleon quickly deleted Cierra's number from his phone and erased her text messages. She'd been the one blowing up his phone. And she wondered why he never tried to commit to her. She was too needy, too desperate. He couldn't respect a woman like that.

Now Maiya was a woman that everybody respected. Although he cheated on her and harbored jealousy against her in his heart, he admired how strong, independent, and determined she was. He equally liked and disliked Maiya's big heart. Nobody, not one person, including him, wanted for anything in her presence. If she was blessed, then so were those around her.

Napoleon sent a text to Cierra, telling her not to use that number again. After he cleared everything pertaining to her and all his other lovers from his phone, he walked over to Maiya and boldly placed the device on the arm of the chair.

"I don't know what you think is going on, but I'm not cheating. To prove it, here is my phone. Keep it. You're going to feel crazy when you realize I haven't done anything. I love you, Maiya. Don't destroy us." Although she didn't answer, he knew that she was listening because her body stiffened and she stopped praying at his nearness.

Napoleon walked away wearing a smug smile, confident that none of his lovers would call that phone today. He was going to send them his new private number.

As for Maiya…

She'll come around. She always does, Napoleon thought, heading back upstairs. It was time to send out that new number and get dressed for his busy day of meetings.

* * * * *

Once Maiya was alone again, she got up and took her first dose of medicine. Then she went into the nearest downstairs bathroom to wash her face. She'd been praying and crying under that blanket. She cried because she was hurt. She prayed because she was mad as hell and needed extra strength to keep from killing this man. She was really struggling to control her anger in this situation and she needed God's help.

As she returned to the chair, Napoleon's phone started ringing again. This time it played his general ringtone. The number registered as private.

Maiya tried to ignore the phone. By the fifth ring, she yanked the phone to her ear and answered it. "Hello?"

"Who is this?" an angry woman replied.

"Who is *this*?" Maiya echoed, feeling her mind go into overdrive as red flags appeared everywhere in her spirit.

"I'm Cierra Hanson – Napoleon's fiancée."

"Oh really? Well, I'm his *wife*."

"Wow! Dwayne told me he was married. After he followed Napoleon over to my house last night and then waited for him to leave, he told me all about your sham of a marriage and a lot of other things. One of which is the fact that they are lovers too. I have the pictures to prove it," Cierra informed, setting off all kinds of bombs.

Maiya shook her head and clenched the phone in a death grip. Things had just gotten real.

CHAPTER FIFTEEN
He Loves Her?

Oh my God! Can this really be true? Was he with her last night or was he with another man? Possibly both? Jesus! Maiya thought in dismay. She held the phone in complete silence a few more moments, trying to gather her composure after such a huge shock.

"Listen, young lady. I don't quite know what's going on here, but I'm about to get to the bottom of it right now," Maiya forced out of her mouth. She was ready to slam the phone down and then hunt Napoleon down like the dog that he obviously was.

"I'm telling you what's going on," Cierra insisted. "I'm his fiancée. I'm wearing his ring. I was just with him last night. Matter of fact, I was with him in Chicago too. Dwayne is obviously his other lover, which means he's been cheating on us both."

Chicago. Maiya cringed at that city name. Napoleon just returned from Chicago a few weeks ago. He was supposed to be conducting a revival up there. Now it appears as though he was doing a lot of other things and a lot of other people there too.

Maiya leaned on the arm of the chair, floored by all she heard and was still hearing. The more Cierra talked, the more evident it became that she was also broken at the hands of Napoleon. It infuriated her to know that while she was ministering to broken people, her husband was creating them.

"I can't believe Napoleon actually married you," Cierra wailed. "That he's been married to you all this time and constantly lying about it. I should have listened to my friend when she told me about seeing y'all together at a conference in Rhode Island. I told Monique it was just a coincidence. That you just had the same last name. When I asked Napoleon about it, he said he didn't even know you. That you were just one of many preachers on the program that day. How dare he lie to me!" She screamed.

Maiya winced at that loud sound. "Honey, that's what liars do – lie," she said through clenched teeth, pulling the phone a few inches from her ear in case the woman screamed again.

"But then again, maybe *you're* the liar," Cierra said, revealing how unstable she was as her emotions and conversation instantly switched directions. "Maybe you and Dwayne are both lying. He could have doctored up those pictures. He could have photo-shopped Napoleon in. I cannot believe this. I *refuse* to believe it. I need to talk to Napoleon. He'll straighten this out. Let me talk to Napoleon. Now!" she yelled furiously.

I've heard enough! Maiya thought, abruptly ending the call. She wasn't about to entertain the foolish rantings of her husband's mistress any longer. Her time would be better spent dealing with him – the cause of all this drama.

Drama, Maiya thought. She shuddered as a forgotten dream flashed before her eyes. She shook her head slowly as vivid memories of that nighttime vision came flooding back to her. In that dream, another local pastor told her that marrying Napoleon would bring more drama to her life than she'd ever had.

"Jesus, why did I miss that? And look at me now," Maiya said, still shaking her head. She blew out a deep breath and covered her face with her hands. "It's my fault." She sounded defeated to her own ears.

Lord, what did I want or need so bad from this marriage, that I missed what You were clearly telling me? Maiya pondered.

Finding her feet again, she made her way to the staircase. She stopped short at the bottom stair as unexplainable pain and rage welled up in her like never before. If she lifted one foot to that stair, she knew she wouldn't stop until she'd gone up there and killed him. Not figuratively, but literally.

Tossing the phone to the floor, Maiya turned around and headed for the door. She grabbed her purse and keys along the way. Thoroughly flustered now, she no longer wanted to talk to or see Napoleon. All she wanted now was to go!

"Lord, how in the world am I flying all over this world ministering to people and my stuff tore up at the house?" Maiya said, talking to the Lord out loud. "How did I miss it again? God, I thought after the foolishness with Cheryl in Chicago and after the women all over the internet, that we had grown past this point, that he was faithful."

Another blunt reminder of that dream sent electrical jolts through her, causing her to shiver. *Lord Jesus, it's all my fault,* she reiterated again. *And now this girl...Lord, this is another hot mess,* she thought, convinced that Cierra had fallen into the same trap as Cheryl.

However, Cheryl had known that Napoleon was married. She was just waiting on him to fulfill his promise to divorce Maiya and marry her. She wanted the status she thought she'd gain by being married to a preacher of his caliber. She revealed that much to Napoleon when he finally told her he was going to work on his marriage and wouldn't see her anymore.

Cheryl, Cierra, different women, same tragedy, Maiya thought, getting into her car.

Though she'd been quick about entering the vehicle, she sat still for a few moments once she was inside. She had to compose herself enough to back out of the garage and get on the road.

Maiya drove with tears streaming down her face. Her mind raced a million miles a second. She didn't call anyone and didn't go see anyone. She just drove...and drove...and drove.

Her mind went back to all those women that Napoleon had chatted with over the years. Some of them he even met from online sites. It was so many. They were almost nameless to her.

Flashes of the piles of emails and instant messages that she printed out flooded her internal vision. Even then that man didn't want to admit what he was doing. But through all of that Maiya forgave Napoleon. She loved him. Now here she was again!

"Lord Jesus, have mercy. I just don't understand," Maiya prayed, continuing to drive around town. "Seriously, Lord, I'm giving him more than he can handle. Well, at least I thought I was," she said, expressing anger and hurt simultaneously.

Incidents like these made her question everything about her womanhood. They made her wonder if something was wrong with her abilities as a wife.

"Lord, I believed him. I believed this raggedy, trifling ass man," she said, slamming her hands against the steering wheel as she reverted back to something she used to do extremely well – cursing. Correction, cussing, because that was how gutter she used to get with her mouth.

Maiya learned a long time ago that life situations can draw you closer to God or cause you to fall back in many ways. Today she allowed herself to fall back into foul language. It was a quick way to release some of her stress and it was a reminder that just because she chose not to do it before, didn't mean she wasn't capable of doing it now. Plus cursing just felt good to her flesh right now.

"I could just kill this bastard. I have put everything on the line. I have taken on raising his children. I trusted mine to him. I shared everything with this man! Oooooh, I could just choke the life out of him!" She minced her words to refrain from going overboard with the cursing, but she beat her poor steering wheel half to death as she pounded on it repeatedly.

"I can't take this NO MORE! I'm sick of this bull...and I'm DONE!" Maiya screamed to the top of her voice to absolutely nobody but God, although He could hear her softest internal whisper. "I admit now that I didn't heed the warning, but, God, I am done! I'm not doing this with him anymore," she said, acknowledging her fault in this seemingly unending nightmare.

Maiya's phone started ringing. She didn't have to look at it to see who was calling. *Free Yourself* was playing, which meant it had to be Napoleon. She assigned this ringtone to his calls in light of the recent revelations concerning him.

Maiya didn't answer the phone. She just let it ring. After he called six more times without getting an answer, the text messages and voicemails started.

"Lady, just call me. I need to talk to you. I came back downstairs and you were gone. I saw my phone at the bottom of the steps. What's going on now? Please don't tell me you're still thinking I gave you a STD. I promise you, I'm not doing anything this time. I don't know what's going on, but somebody is setting me up," he continued to lie on the voicemail she listened to.

"Are you serious? You have got to be kidding me?" Maiya said, feeling extremely weak in her spirit. "I know his raggedy ass is not saying this crap. I'm so serious when I say I'm done with his *ass!*"

That second curse word seemed to echo in the car, causing her to really hear herself in that heated moment. She dropped her head in shame, realizing that she was giving him power over her that he didn't deserve.

In an instant, Maiya decided to do everything within her power to control her anger and her tongue. She knew the ramifications could be less than favorable if she didn't. Thus she didn't say anything for a while. She just kept driving in silence, stopping briefly to gas up the car again.

"Jesus, give me strength. I do not believe this. I have forgiven him more times than I care to remember and I just can't do this anymore," Maiya said when she trusted herself to speak again.

The phone started ringing once more. She sent it straight to voicemail and refused to listen to it. She didn't want to hear Napoleon's voice again. Ever! The phone kept ringing back to back, reigniting her smoldering anger.

Two hours later, she finally answered his call. "What!" she barked out.

"Lady, where are you, baby? What's going on? Why did you leave again? I came down to try to talk and you weren't here. I thought if I gave you some time and left my phone with you, you would see that I'm not cheating. Baby, please come back so we can talk this through," Napoleon said, trying to sound genuine yet again.

Maiya didn't say anything in response. She simply laid the phone down on the passenger seat and kept driving.

"Lady?"

She could hear him, but she allowed silence to be her answer. Inside she boiled with rage about him calling her the reverential name used by members of their former church.

"Okay look, Lady. I don't know what's going on here, but if you don't tell me, I can't help."

"Napoleon, you can be sure of this one thing, I am NOT your lady and I don't want you to fix anything," she said, not bothering to pick up the phone as she gripped the steering wheel tighter. "What you can do is stop calling me and stop talking to me. You can get your stuff, everything you brought into the house and get the hell out!" she yelled through clenched teeth.

By now Maiya was hanging on by a thread. Her thoughts were assaulting her like a jagged edge knife cutting flesh. Anger kept spewing through her as rapidly as a mountain of lava on the verge of erupting. Bitterness scraped across her soul like nails on a chalk board.

Maiya knew she was about to blow up! She couldn't hold it any longer. She refused to.

"I don't want to hear your lies," she said, shouting loud enough for him to hear her. "I'm not listening to you blame the woman, you can sell that bull to someone who is buying. You have gone too far and this time, I am not, hear me good, NOT taking you back. It's over!" Maiya's vision suddenly blurred. She swerved quickly to keep from hitting another car.

"Lady, what the hell are you talking about? Why are you telling me to leave? What the hell is going on with you? What woman are you talking about?" Napoleon sounded angry with her now.

"Cierra!" Maiya spat out.

This time silence came from Napoleon.

Click!

Maiya hung up in his face. Then she pulled her car over to the side of the road and parked. She had to get herself together. She needed to calm down enough to drive back home, which was where she decided to go…eventually.

* * * * *

Thirty minutes later, Maiya restarted the car and drove back to the house. She rode in silence as she continued to steady her choppy breathing and slow down her racing thoughts.

Once she arrived at her destination, she found the garage door still open. She forgot to close it earlier in her haste.

I wonder if he knows that it's still open, Maiya thought, parking her vehicle.

Obviously not. She answered her own question a few seconds later as she entered the family room and heard Napoleon engrossed in deep conversation. She stood perfectly still just outside the kitchen doorway, watching and listening in silence as he talked openly to someone using the speaker feature of his cell phone.

He's so stupid, Maiya surmised, listening to him sprout utter foolishness as he moved frantically around the kitchen.

Napoleon appeared infuriated. His tone was rough and he kept hitting the kitchen counter as he read through his text messages.

She watched him end one call and continue reading his text messages while he called someone else. A female someone else.

"Cierra!" Napoleon yelled into the phone as soon as she answered. "Why did you—"

"Napoleon, I've been calling you over and over again," Cierra interrupted. "I need to talk to you. I want to know why you said you were preaching at that Rhode Island conference when you weren't. Monique told me it was your wife preaching that day. Your *wife*! You told me you weren't married, but when I called your phone today, she answered. So what do you have to say now? You said you didn't even know her." She screamed in frustration. "And Dwayne told me that you are definitely married to her, so don't even start lying. You said you loved me. *Me*!" She burst out in tears.

Napoleon suddenly calmed. He smirked. His face took on a sly, serpent-like expression. His eyes looked calculating.

"Listen, listen, listen, baby," he said soothingly. "I'm not married to that woman...anymore. I used to be married to her and I know I should have told you. Look, baby, she came over today as I was getting ready to take a shower. I had no idea she was going to pick up my phone. I admit she was at the conference and she did preach, but I didn't know she was going to be there. Baby, what makes you think I'm still married to her? And who is Dwayne? Girl, what are you talking about? I don't know anybody named Dwayne. Besides, baby, Maiya is gay. That's why we're not together anymore. She doesn't even like my kind. Lady, you're the only one I want," Napoleon spoke hurriedly, further revealing his guilt. He always spoke in a rushed tone when he was lying.

"Then why was she there? And y'all just happen to have the same last name? Man, you must think I'm stupid?" Cierra yelled even more through her tears.

"Baby, baby. No, I know you're not stupid. Lady, come on now. I just told you about her. She's a stalker. She just showed up over here today out of the blue. Baby, she's gone now. That's why I'm on the phone with you," Napoleon said, revealing something else that Clueless Cierra missed.

How stupid can they both be? Maiya thought. *He's on the phone with her, because he thinks I'm not here.*

"Baby, listen, I'm coming back over tonight and we'll straighten all this out then. I'm going to get between those honey lips and make you forget all about this. You know how you like these lips on you. Come on, Pookie Poo. Don't let some crazy lady mess up your good thing," he said, wagging his tongue.

Maiya cringed at that sight. She forced herself to remain quiet and still when she really wanted to murder-death-kill him like a scene out of *Demolition Man.*

"I—" Cierra begin.

"Listen, baby, just calm down," Napoleon interrupted, dominating the conversation now. "Daddy's gonna call you back in just a little bit. I love you. I know how you like that sweet talk. I'm gonna call you back and give you all you can take. I'll call you on Face Time and you can stroke it for me."

Oh, that is just disgusting right there! He loves her? Really? Maiya shook her head.

"I love you too and you better call me back," Cierra replied, calming all the way down to mush.

Crushed even further now, Maiya sat down in the nearest chair. She felt weak and nauseated. Humiliation held hands with her anger. She wasn't sure what to say or do for that matter. So many things were going through her mind, scenarios of how this could play out. For a few moments, her mind just went blank.

Hanging up the phone, Napoleon walked into the family room where Maiya sat. He stumbled when he saw the door leading to the garage standing open. His head snapped around until his eyes lit upon her. He quickly hid the startled look on his face and walked toward her.

Maiya had no idea what he was thinking, but she could guarantee it was not what she was thinking. *I ought to blow his brains out! This Negro got some damn nerve. After all the days and night I spent nursing his black ass back to health when he was sick. All the money I spent getting him out of jail for stupid stuff. He got life messed up if he thinks it's about to be all good. Oh hell naw! If he walks up on me, I'm gonna beat the black off of him!*

With her thoughts racing and her anger boiling over, Maiya knew she was about to do something irrational if she didn't bring her mind back in line. She had to regain control quickly, lest this turn out worse than it already was. She bowed her head and took in a deep breath.

"I heard everything," she said, snapping her head back up.

Fear instantly registered in Napoleon's eyes. He tripped over his own feet and backed up quickly. He knew he was caught.

CHAPTER SIXTEEN
Just Walk Away

Although Napoleon clearly knew that he was caught, Maiya knew there was no way he was going to admit his guilt. It just didn't seem to be in him to do so. Fortunately, he was wise enough to leave some distance between them.

I should have stayed gone. I could have gone to Mama Ludie's house, a hotel or somewhere. Anywhere else but here, Maiya thought, not hearing a word Napoleon said as he once again tried to explain away the truth. She was in a daze. Everything was becoming a blur to her.

Times like these she really missed her grandmother. But Momma had already gone to glory several years ago.

Napoleon continued to talk. What little Maiya did hear from his mouth was sickening to her. The more she heard, the more she despised him and the fake horse he rode into her life on.

"Lady, baby, come on now. We have to talk. I don't know what is going on here. I don't even know anyone named Cierra. Baby, please tell me what's going on," Napoleon said, hooding his eyes with his naturally long eyelashes.

Maiya didn't respond as he continued his tirade of lies on top of lies. She dropped her head, because the sight of him made her sick. She felt like throwing up in her mouth.

"Listen, are you going to at least tell me why you left and why you wouldn't answer my calls. I cancelled all my meetings today just for you. Baby, I'm trying here, but you're making this so hard. I'm a faithful husband. I only want you. There's no one else I could even think of being with besides you. Baby, please say something. It's killing me that you won't even look at me. Please, *please* talk to me. Whatever it is, we can get through this. We're the dream team."

Suddenly the man actually started crying. Crying! For real?

Just as quickly Maiya blew her gasket. All of her cool went out the window, the door and everywhere else as she pounced upon him without warning. Her right fist flew clean across his face so hard that it caused him to fall backward.

She went from saying nothing at all to screaming to the top of her lungs until even she didn't understand what she was saying. She slung fast punches, right and left hooks. Napoleon never had a chance to recover from the first blow before she cold clocked him upside the head with more.

"Shut the hell up talking to me! All this time, you've been claiming to be out ministering and preaching. Instead you've been sleeping with another woman. Do you really think I'm that stupid? Well, stupid just checked out, partna!" With each word, she landed another blow to his body.

Napoleon couldn't control her, though he tried. Every time he attempted to grab her hands, she was too quick for him. Finally he snatched her entire frame up from the floor and pinned her against the nearest wall.

"Maiya, if you hit me again, it's not going to be pretty. I said I'm not cheating. I said I didn't give you no damn STD. And you hauled off and hit me? Don't hit me again, I'm warning you," Napoleon fumed.

POW!

That was the sound Maiya's right hand made when she slapped fire off Napoleon's face, causing him to drop her to the floor. "I heard your sorry ass! I just heard you on the phone too, so save that. Save it forever because I'm not interested!"

Napoleon reached for her, but she quickly moved away. When he stepped forward and reached for her again, she pushed his hands away to stop him from touching her.

"Do not touch me! Don't you ever even *think* about touching me again! I can't believe I actually believed you. I believed *in* you! I trusted your janky ass and *this* is the repayment I get? Napoleon Tulane Jackson, get your punk ass out of my house and get out NOW!" So enraged, she felt as if her blood was actually boiling.

"*Your* house?" Napoleon shouted.

"Yes, you heard me right – *my* house, *my* deed, and *my* mortgage payment. It's all mine – M.I.N.E.! Just because everyone else doesn't know the truth, don't you dare stand there and act like you don't. I wish you would!" Maiya said, reminding him of something he wanted to keep secret. The same something that she never said to him until today. She kept quiet even when he boasted to his buddies about buying the house for her. No more protecting him now. He hadn't bothered to protect himself or her when he was out whoring around.

"Yeah, well the law says I have a right to be here," Napoleon replied, looking glad to be off the original subject that started this whole fight.

"I don't care what the law says. I want you and your lies out of here! The nerve of you actually getting engaged to another woman while you're still married to me," she said, steering the conversation back to the real issue. She wasn't about to let him off the hook that easily.

"Lady, what are you talking about—"

Maiya interrupted his words with another punch, causing him to fall to the floor. Her temper was beyond out of control as she put her right foot in the center of his stomach.

"How...how can I possibly be engaged to someone and I'm married to you? Why would you even listen to whoever you say this woman is? Well, that's if there is a woman. You...you know how your mind is," he said breathlessly, glaring up at her.

Maiya pressed down harder. In her rage, she didn't give a second thought to his heart and the pacemaker that he'd gotten a year ago.

Suddenly the words '*you know how your mind is*' boomeranged in her soul, prompting something inside of her to snap. Outwardly she calmed completely down, becoming almost too calm for her own self.

Maiya looked down at Napoleon and shook her head. "If you don't get out of my house tonight, it will be your *last* night. If you know anything about me, you know I don't make empty threats. I *will* kill you. That's a promise." Then she turned around, grabbed her purse and marched upstairs.

Maiya entered her bedroom, closed the door, and locked it. While she may have allowed Napoleon to see her fighting mad, she would not allow him to ever see her shed another tear. He'd seen too many already and apparently it meant nothing to him. This time she'd cry alone, though he was not worthy of a single tear that streamed down her face.

* * * * *

Maiya paced the floor in her room for hours, waiting on God to comfort her. She heard the garage closing under her. She hoped he'd left, but unfortunately at some point during the night, Napoleon posted up outside the bedroom door.

He talked all kinds of nonsense that never penetrated her soul. She kept the door closed and didn't say a word. She knew the danger. She could see it very clearly. She knew that opening that door would open up something deadly in both of their lives, especially since he had yet to leave the house in his desperation to cling to her and the lifestyle that came along with her.

After all those years of trying to make it work, of forgiving and not holding grudges. Here we go all over again, Maiya thought, continuing to pace the floor.

By the time her pacing and crying stopped, she had made a pivotal decision – she would trust God to carry her through this and shield her from any subsequent fallout. Ministry or no ministry, Napoleon had to go.

Maiya would finally and fully embrace the scriptures that allowed her to walk away from this known adulterer and this toxic relationship.

Around midnight, Napoleon began a long spill about Cierra. All of a sudden, he remembered knowing her. "Okay, okay, okay. I admit it. I met the woman named Cierra, but I didn't know she was crazy, baby. This woman has been stalking me for months and I've been trying to break it off. But every time I tried, she threatened to tell you. I just didn't know how to get out of it. I swear to you it didn't mean anything. Baby, I'm sorry. I just didn't want to lose you. You've been here so many times through so many things. I know I've done this before, but I swear I'll never do it again. I just couldn't stop. Maiya, say something please."

Maiya remained mute as she sat on the floor beside the bed. Her purse lay beside her. The tears had long since stopped. Now she just stared at the wall, trying to figure out how in the world she missed the signs this time.

Maiya knew she was not a perfect woman or wife. But she'd been gracious to Napoleon and she'd loved him completely. When he needed her, she was there. When he wanted her, she made herself available. When he was sick, she shut everyone and everything down to care for him.

So while she was not perfect, she did right by that man. More so than any other man she could think of. This last incident pushed her back over the edge to a place she struggled to recover from many years ago. It hurt, plain and simple. Deep down in her soul it hurt.

Napoleon was right about one thing. He had done this several times before. Certainly enough times for Maiya to keep her eyes wide open this time.

Was she that much in love that she became blind to his perpetually cheating ways? Or did she see them, then simply ignored them because she couldn't deal with all this again?

Maiya didn't have a ready answer to either of those questions. Instead she prayed. Cursing and fighting weren't going to work. She'd been there and done that too much over the last twenty-four hours.

Lord, forgive me and have mercy, Maiya prayed.

"Listen, love, we can get through this," Napoleon continued outside the bedroom door. "You're the best thing that has ever happened to me. Baby, I can call Cierra right now and tell her with you listening to never call me again. She can't use it against me anymore because now you know. Baby, just open the door so I can hold you. I can make this right. I will never jeopardize our love again. Let me in. I need you. I need to make love to you. Let me get between those honey lips like you like it. I can make all this disappear, if you just open the door."

What! Maiya thought, seeing red all over again. She couldn't believe this man had the audacity to say the same thing to her that he recently told ol' girl.

Inwardly, she heard the still quiet voice of God again. *Don't negatively alter your life because of someone else. It will work out for your good.*

Taking that as a sign for her to leave rather than go through the potential violent trouble of *making* him leave, Maiya stood to her feet with her purse in hand. After making sure the black leather bag contained her keys, medication, and cell phone, she quickly went down the alternate stairwell.

"Maiya," Napoleon called out to her.

Silence.

"Maiya?"

More silence.

"Maiya!" he said louder.

The woman in question was gone. After running downstairs, she quickly fled the house...*her* house...that she absolutely loved. If it were not for the sound of the garage opening, Napoleon would have never known she was gone.

As Maiya drove down the street, she saw the front door of the house swing open and him running out. He ran fast for a man with a pacemaker. He did a lot of things for a man with a pacemaker...but he couldn't catch her as she sped away.

When Maiya rounded the corner of her block, her phone started ringing. This time she turned it completely off. She could not deal with any more lies tonight. She couldn't deal with anything actually. Her body was tired, her mind and heart were overwhelmed and she needed to shut down.

Maiya drove to Centennial Park, parked the car and walked around for a while. So out of it, she didn't think about safety. No place felt safe to her at that point. She just wanted to be in a place that brought her peace. For her, it was the beach or the park. Since the park was closer, she came here.

Maybe I should have kept driving to the beach, Maiya thought. But then again, no amount of distance would have been far enough to remove the pain she felt.

Maiya walked through the park for hours or so it seemed. The whole thing played over and over in her head. She couldn't understand how she missed everything that was right in front of her face.

Why didn't I see it? Oh you saw it all right, she chided herself. *And God even sent you a dream,* she thought, angrier now.

Times past began to play in Maiya's mind. Flashbacks were plentiful now. One in particular stood out from an experience she thought she'd never get over. It happened in Tennessee. A local woman there had claimed to be engaged to Napoleon too.

"Lord Jesus, I must be the stupid one. That girl said some of the same things as Cierra." Maiya couldn't recall the Tennessee woman's name now. However, she did remember the drama the woman brought with her.

Vividly.

They were at a church service when Miss Tennessee suddenly burst right down the center aisle and went stone crazy just as Napoleon was about to preach. She yelled about him being with her the weekend before and about him having the nerve to bring Maiya to church that day when they were supposed to be getting married.

Lord, Lord, Lord. This really wasn't hidden from me. I overlooked it! Maiya recalled, still wrestling with her thoughts.

That was just one instance of Napoleon's infidelity. She couldn't even begin to recount how many more there were or how many women had come out of the woodwork over the seven years they'd been together. Looking back now, she didn't know why she stayed with him all this time.

Never again! Maiya's mind was made up and there was no turning back.

Looking upward, her eyes were drawn to the Omni Hotel sign right across the street from the park. Seeing that image as a divine sign from above, she got in her car and went to reserve a room for several nights.

Maiya rarely left that room for anything. She didn't bother to go home to get any clothes. She simply bought new ones. She called her children daily so they wouldn't worry and to keep in contact with them. Other than that, she didn't call anyone else or answer any calls, preferring to shut herself off from the world while she cried, prayed and tried to decide how she was going to move on with her life.

Six days later, Maiya ventured out of her emotional shutdown long enough to call her assistant. Angie didn't question her. She just listened.

Maiya talked for almost twenty minutes straight, revealing how she didn't know which direction to go in ministry-wise. She knew exactly what she was going to do about her marriage – get out.

"Put a halt to everything right now. There's no way I can keep doing ministry like this. I'm not in any mental, emotional, or spiritual position to be ministering to others right now," Maiya said, thinking about the welfare of God's precious sheep. They must be protected at all costs. Every good under-shepherd knew this. Hirelings didn't care and she was no hireling.

Angie remained quiet as she vented. "First and foremost, I love you. Take all the time you need. Everything is covered," she finally said. "Call Van. I'll take care of everyone else."

"Okay. Thanks and I love you too." Maiya smiled for the first time in a week. Calling Angie had been a good idea.

After they concluded their call, she got up and showered instead of calling Van right away. She wasn't ready to talk to anyone else just yet. When she was refreshed, she put on some clothes, crawled onto the plush sofa lounger in the room and finally made that promised call.

"Where are you? I'm coming to get you," Van said as soon as he picked up the phone. "It's Maiya," he whispered to Janine, who must have been nearby.

Maiya smiled again, grateful that he was always so protective of her. She built him up during some of the roughest times of his life and he returned the favor a hundredfold. Fortunately, his wife not only understood their relationship, but encouraged and supported it. Janine became a good friend as well over the years, especially after Maiya helped save their marriage.

"I'm at the Omni Hotel across from Centennial Park. Room 627," Maiya replied. She knew there was no need to argue with Van. She really didn't want to. It was time to face people again, at least the ones that she trusted.

"I'm on my way," Van said.

Maiya heard him tell Janine where he was going before he hung up. That made her smile again.

Unfortunately, that smile didn't last long. Maiya's tears quickly returned after she concluded the call. They expressed things she couldn't verbalize at the time. She really didn't have any words to say. She couldn't think of anything prolific to pray. She felt lost all over again.

Almost a half hour later, Van knocked on the door. "Maiya, it's me. Open up," he said in a gentle tone.

She got up, wiping her face as she made her way over to the locked door.

"Don't worry, we got you." Van drew her into his arms as soon as she opened the door and let him in. He didn't just hug her, he also prayed for her.

Maiya didn't say anything. She just stood there and let him minister to her. "I'm not going back to that house," she whispered against his chest when the fervent prayer was over.

"Fine with me," Van said. Then after packing up the few belongings she had in the room, he took her back to his house where Janine awaited to assist with any physical needs that Maiya had.

Meanwhile, Angie called the rest of the team and let them know that Maiya was fine and that they were to continue working on the plans for the conference. She gave additional instructions concerning the other projects, including the upcoming book release. Additional dates were set up for them to meet.

Most importantly, Angie expressed the urgency and need for them to keep praying not just for Maiya, but for the entire ministry.

CHAPTER SEVENTEEN
Seeing Is Something Different

Maiya slept in late the next day. She didn't wake up until well after 2pm. By then Van and Janine had gone to the hotel to get her vehicle. They did a little shopping on the way back.

Janine stopped by several local boutiques to get Maiya more changing clothes. She knew exactly what sizes to get and she was familiar with her fashion sense. Van went to the grocery store to get some of Maiya's favorite foods. All of that equated to love in action, which she highly appreciated and needed at a time like this.

Maiya took her time returning home. After staying with Van and Janine for five days, she still refused to go back. She wasn't ready yet. Fortunately, they didn't force the issue with her, though Van did broach the subject in order to keep her from going deeper into depression.

Janine quickly shut that conversation down by reminding him of the time she left home and needed to come to terms with things in her own time. That was enough to keep Van silent for a while and just trust God that Maiya would eventually come all the way out of shutdown mode.

Ten days later, Maiya decided that it was time to go back home. She opted to return alone, despite Van's protests otherwise. She felt ready...until she walked into the family room.

"Well I'll be—" was the first thing out of her mouth before she slammed it shut. She looked around in shock.

Napoleon was gone all right. But did he have to take the entire family room with him?

"I know the hell this fool didn't take all my stuff," Maiya said, unable to believe her eyes as she slowly scanned the room from left to right.

When she was sure that her eyes weren't deceiving her, she walked farther into the house. Entering the formal living room, she saw that all of the brand new furniture was gone as well. She went to the back of the house in disbelief only to find that the kitchen table and chairs were gone too. The only things left were the four high-back, leather bar stools.

"Ain't this about some bull?" Maiya shook her head. "This dude right here. Jesus, help me," she prayed.

She immediately rushed upstairs to see what else he'd taken, if anything. The first place she went to was her bedroom. The bed was still intact. So were all the other furnishings.

She turned and went to check the other bedrooms. That lowdown scoundrel had taken all of the furniture from one of the guestrooms, including the large TV. That room was literally bare wall to wall, just like he left the family room. He took the bed and a dresser from another guestroom.

Maiya ran to the children's rooms to investigate. "Well, at least he left their rooms intact," she said, only partially relieved that he wasn't as trifling as she thought. She shook her head thinking about all the other rooms he plundered.

"I cannot believe he would stoop this low. I'm about to call him," she raged, returning to her bedroom. "No, Maiya, don't. It's not going to make it better," she told herself, attempting to calm down.

Though grateful that the house hadn't been cleaned out entirely, Maiya still couldn't let go of the devastation of what he had taken. "What kind of person...no, what kind of *man* would do something like that?" She shook her head again as she sat on the side of the bed. She remained glued to that spot until the shock wore off.

After willfully calming herself down, Maiya decided to take a shower. Though she'd taken one before arriving, it was relaxing to her. Napoleon's low down deeds made *her* feel tense. They made her feel tired, too. All she wanted to do now was relax, lie down and sleep.

A small part of her still wanted to call and curse him out again, but she refrained. She simply lacked the energy. It took everything in her to remove the cell phone from her purse. Besides, she didn't really want to hear his voice right now or ever for that matter.

Maiya heard enough of Napoleon's voice during her absence. Those sad sob messages he left on her voicemail had been more than gag worthy. One message said, "I'm just going to leave, because you don't want me anymore."

Another one said, "I won't bother you again, but you need to check yourself. It's all your fault."

Napoleon even had the nerve to leave a message that said, "You're not as good of a wife as you think you are. That's why I cheated. Even still I'm really sorry this time and want to make it work."

"Blah, blah, blah! What the hell ever!" Maiya shouted, remembering all the crap he'd left on her voicemail as she rose to her feet, leaving her phone on the bed.

She could feel her blood pressure rising again as she undressed down to her undies. Her anger, which boiled just beneath the surface, was still very real. So was the rage inside of her.

On the way to the bathroom, Maiya stopped at the linen closet to grab her favorite towel and a few other things. When she opened the door, her heart dropped. Her mouth hung open. That clown took all the towels, robes, soap, and bathroom supplies!

Adrenaline rushed through Maiya's body as she ran back into her bedroom and slung her other closet doors open. Her suits, hats, shoes, and purses were gone. All of them! Everything! Some of the items still had tags on them due to her shopping addiction. Maiya loved suits and especially shoes. She bought them in droves – two, three and four pairs at a time. Napoleon knew this and had taken them all.

"Okay, I don't believe this sorry …." Maiya paused, placed her hands on her throbbing temples and took a deep breath. "This man really took my clothes. Okay, now I'm really gonna call his ass!"

She stomped across the room and snatched her phone from the bed. She took in more deep breaths to try to steady her breathing while she waited for him to pick up.

"Hel-lo," Napoleon answered in a singsong tone.

"Napoleon, why the hell did you take *my* stuff out of this house?"

"I said I would leave and you're still not happy," he replied smugly.

"That furniture doesn't belong to you! TV's, beds and my clothes! Are you serious? What man steals a woman's clothes?" Maiya said sharply.

He laughed wickedly.

"What the hell is so funny?" she yelled, incensed by his laughter and the nerve of him to do so. "I *knew* I should have taken a magnet to your ass, drained the life out of that pacemaker *and* you!"

"Too late for that now. Oh, you must have missed the refrigerator and the freezer too." His tone was as cold as the freezer he mentioned. "You ain't seen nothing yet. When I get done with you, there will be no you, Prophetess," he said mockingly.

With the phone in hand, Maiya flew downstairs, taking two at a time. When she finally made it to the kitchen, she stopped and looked around. The refrigerator was right where she left it.

"What in the world is this fool talking about?" she wondered out loud, heading for the closest garage where the deep freezer was kept. It was still there too.

She suddenly felt an unction to open it. Following that leading, she lifted the top of the freezer and found it E.M.P.T.Y!

Running back into the kitchen, Maiya snatched the door open and found it empty as well. She turned around in circles for a moment in total delusion. She had to be losing it!

"What the hell, Napoleon?" She yanked the phone back up to her right ear, only to find that he had already hung up.

Maiya stood next to the kitchen island half-naked in her bra and panties, feeling and no doubt looking like a first class fool. He took two TV's, two beds, about four dressers and all the furniture on the first floor. To top it off, he took her clothes and of all things, the groceries.

"Are you freaking kidding me right now?" Maiya said furiously, slamming her hand down on the counter. "I'm not even going to pretend like I'm not mad because I am. This man has got to be out of his mind." She dialed his number again.

Of course, he didn't answer this time. The coward!

The man had given her an STD, cheated more times than she could remember, asked two other women to marry him while he was married to her and now he'd stolen from her. No reality show could top all this drama.

"I swear if I write this, somebody would put it on TV," Maiya said in absolute disbelief. "This is borderline scandal!" She'd never seen anything like this in all her life.

Maiya moved over to one of the remaining bar stools and sat down. Her mind reeled like a ship at sea. She had difficulty holding a clear thought.

"Lord, have mercy." The tears started to fall again. There were no prolific words or prayers, only a heartfelt, "Lord, have mercy." Sometimes that was all that was needed.

Mercy came in the form of sleep.

* * * * *

Maiya woke up the next morning to a continuously ringing phone. At least she thought it was the next morning. Her bedroom was dark and the sun hadn't come up yet.

My God! What in the world? How did I get up here? Maiya thought, unable to recall ever leaving the kitchen bar stool.

Had an angel carried her upstairs? Stranger things had happened in her life. Thanks to Napoleon, she was almost living her own *Nightmare on Elm Street.*

"And who keeps ringing my phone?" She groggily sat up in bed and reached on the nightstand where the phone normally was. She groaned in irritation when she didn't feel it there.

When the persistent device rang again from somewhere down near her waist, Maiya felt around in the bed for it. "Hello?" she said, pulling the phone up to her right ear. Her eyes remained closed.

"May I speak to Lady Jackson?" It wasn't what the male caller said, but *how* he said it that alerted her to trouble. He sounded like he was about to break out in laughter.

"This is Maiya. Who is this?" She rubbed the back of her neck and rotated it slightly, trying to ease some of the tension she felt from the pounding in her head.

"This is Dwayne."

"Okay, Dwayne. How can I help you?" she said, wondering if this was the same Dwayne from the conference center. It certainly sounded like him.

"Well, I have some information that I'm sure you'll want," he said quickly.

"Is this Dwayne from the conference center?" Maiya asked just to be sure. If it was, how did he get her personal number? She knew Angie would never give it out. Had Allysa done so? They had seemed overly friendly with one another that day at the front desk.

Something's not right here, Maiya discerned, opening her eyes.

"Yes, it is," was his smug reply. "I've got something for you."

"Oh, is this about the venue? If so, please contact my assistant and she'll handle anything needed," Maiya said, eager to end the call. The last thing she wanted to talk about was ministry stuff. "Her number is—"

"That's not why I called," Dwayne interrupted. "I have something to tell you about Napoleon."

Maiya sighed heavily. "Whatever you need to say about Napoleon, say it to him. I don't have time to entertain it."

"Oh no, ma'am. He doesn't want to hear this and I know he doesn't want *you* to hear it either. But after what he's done, it's too late. I'm telling you and everybody else. That includes his sisters, his children, *and* the church. I'm telling every damn body, every damn thing," he said very angrily.

Maiya heard the rage in his voice. Simultaneously she realized that this wasn't just Dwayne from the conference center, but also the same Dwayne that Cierra spoke of. Dwayne – owner of some supposedly incriminating pictures. Dwayne – Napoleon's alleged other lover.

How could she have possibly forgotten all that? Shock had clouded her memory. Also disbelief since that damaging report had come from a scorned woman.

"Hold up, son! Hold the hell up right now!" Maiya jumped up from her bed, sliding easily into rarely used slang from yesteryear. "What you ain't gon' to do is mess with my children! You can do whatever you want to do with Napoleon. He ain't my business or concern anymore. But, and I am so serious, you will *not* go anywhere near those children. Whatever your issue is with him, you keep it with him. You don't want to try me. Dude, I promise you, this ain't what you want!" She paced the floor in her rant.

"Look, I'm just trying to tell you what's about to go down. I would've thought that you'd like to know that your man is sleeping *with* a man!" he said bluntly.

Although Cierra alluded to Napoleon's bisexuality, to actually hear it confirmed by the man's lover literally slung Maiya into the wall. She grabbed the door closest to her and leaned on it. It felt like the breath had been punched out of her lungs. Her hands shook. Her eyes felt as if they were about to pop straight out of her head.

"Did you hear me, Prophetess? Your precious Bishop isn't just sleeping with other women. He's been sleeping with me. Me, a M-A-N," he said, spelling out the word in a braggadocios manner.

Once again, Maiya had no words. She couldn't say anything if she wanted to. She had no wind. She couldn't even remain on her feet as she slid down the closet door she leaned against in utter devastation.

"You see, Prophetess," Dwayne continued mockingly. "I'm not just any man, I was *his* man. At least I was until he slept with my girlfriend a few weeks ago. My girlfriend A-lly-sa," he said slowly, breaking up the syllables of her name.

Maiya looked in the diamond-shaped mirror on the wall opposite her and saw torment creep upon her face like a deadly tarantula. Her limbs felt numb. She couldn't hear herself breathing anymore. Yet the phone seemed glued to her hand and her ear.

"Your man and I have been swinging for years and now he wants to pull this bull with me. I guess he forgot that I have proof!" he said too loudly, disrespecting her eardrum and her tormented heart. "As a matter of fact, I sent some of our 'special moments' to your phone. I'm sure you're going to just love them!" Sarcasm laced with malice dripped from his every word. It sounded like a venomous drawl.

Either I'm going crazy or this man is in love with my husband. The same husband that apparently slept with one of my team members, Maiya deduced. The reality of that slammed into her like a ton of bricks.

Jesus! She prayed as her mind flashed back to the last time she saw Allysa. The girl had been flirting with Dwayne at the front desk that day. Dwayne – Allysa's boyfriend and now proud bearer of bad news.

"After all I've been to him and after all we've shared. Oh, I'm not letting this go," Dwayne continued to rant. "He will feel the brunt of what he's done to me. You have no idea what's really been going on. I gave this man everything, even money from my trust fund. I've even paid your house note at times, when he wanted to pretend to pay it just to impress you. And he has the nerve to do this to me? Oh no, ma'am. No, sir! I won't have it. I'm taking him all the way down and anybody who gets in my way is going down too. I thought I'd start with you. He claims he loves you so much and didn't want to hurt you. Well, I don't love you. I love *him* and because of you, he left both of us!" By now he was yelling erratically at her and crying.

What the world am I hearing on this line? Maiya thought. *This is madness. Pure madness!* She almost wanted to laugh because this could not be real. *Stop the music! I have got to be tripping.*

"Oh my God! You are really in love with Napoleon, aren't you?" Maiya asked the scorned man as she slowly came out of her shock. "And did you just say, because of *me*, he left *both* of us?"

"I sure am and I sure did."

"Look, Dwayne, this is all news to me. But regardless of whatever you have or had with him, her, or whoever – Napoleon could have left me a long time ago. I told him the last time he cheated that he could go, but your precious Napoleon begged, cried, and swore that I was the *only* one he wanted," Maiya replied, starting to feel stronger by the second. Her strength was fueled by her rising anger.

"That's the same stuff he told me too. I wonder which one of us got the truth. I guess neither since he's gone now."

"Either way, that man stayed with me because he *wanted* to for whatever reasons, none of which I know at this point," Maiya said. "How long did you say y'all been doing… what you say y'all been doing?" she asked, not sure how to pose that question. The whole thing was confusing to her.

"Three years," Dwayne replied. "And that wench that I'm no longer with because she slept with Napoleon a little bit too easily, she's got something coming to her in about an hour or so. That car Allysa's been riding around in, in *my* name, is being picked up. TODAY!" He screamed, sounding exactly like a female.

Who does this? Maiya was baffled by all the players in this tangled web of lies and deceit. None of them seemed to have any sense in their heads. She had sense, but had acted like a blind Betty for far too long.

"Look, I don't want to hear anymore," Maiya said, snapping back from her thoughts. It was time to stop this man from berating her with unwanted information about her husband. "You need to deal with him. I'm not your issue. I don't want him. You can have him. She can have him. Hell, all y'all can have him." Then she finally hung up, dropping the phone on the floor.

As soon as the call ended, text messages started coming in. They were from Dwayne. Dwayne, who'd kept his promise about sending her those pictures. Hurt, scorned, and rejected Dwayne, who didn't care who he hurt as he lashed out in his own pain.

"Oh God!" Maiya gasped after picking the phone up and opening the first message. Therein were two pictures of Dwayne and Napoleon together in a most primal way. Hearing about their debauchery was one thing, but to actually see it caused another wave of devastation to surge through her.

"Stop it! Cut it out! Noooooo!" Maiya screamed, flinging the phone across the room.

CHAPTER EIGHTEEN
Nothing Left to Lose

After crying for hours, Maiya remained prostrate in the middle of the floor. Her wailing had turned to whimpers and sniffles as she slowly tried to pull herself together. She finally sat up, yet lingering shock kept her sitting on the floor for a little while longer.

Amazingly, her mind wasn't wondering or wandering. She wasn't thinking or praying. The only thing she felt was pain. She just rocked back and forth, holding herself because no one else's arms would do at the moment.

Maiya abruptly jolted up from the floor. She ran to the bathroom, feeling the need to wash away the very thought of having ever been with Napoleon. She couldn't take a shower fast enough now.

"God, I gotta get checked out all over again," she cried, snatching the lingerie from her body and flinging them into the bathroom hamper. She could care less that all the towels were gone. She'd dry herself off with a curtain if she had to. Fortunately, Napoleon hadn't taken her shower gel or favorite loofa, so she had the necessary items to suds up and scrub with.

"Lord Jesus, have mercy," Maiya prayed, continuing to scrub her body.

If only she could scrub away the images that kept flashing in her mind. She desperately tried to, but after seeing that first photo, she had difficulty focusing on anything else. The fact that Napoleon slept with all those people, including a man, and then came home and slept with her was proving to be too much for her.

"Ughhhh," Maiya uttered in disgust. She scrubbed a little harder, trying to remove the extra nastiness she felt in that moment. The harder she scrubbed, the worst she felt.

Leaning against the back wall of the stall, she let the pelting water roll over her. More tears streamed down her face, joining the sudsy water flowing down the drain. After allowing the warm water to soothe her for another ten minutes, she prayed some more and finished her shower.

Maiya felt physically clean after her shower, but her heart was heavy nevertheless. When she heard her phone ringing from the bedroom, she didn't bother to answer it this time. She wasn't in the mood to talk to anyone yet.

After putting on some workout clothes that she found in a dresser drawer, she spent more time in prayer. She had to rebuild her spiritual strength slowly but surely for whatever else waited ahead.

When she felt strong enough, Maiya retrieved her phone and began looking at what Dwayne sent her. She wanted to know everything now. She'd been in the dark long enough.

The things she saw were appalling and yet not unfamiliar in light of her past with Old No-Tooth. If it could be done with a woman or a man, it was in those pictures. Some of them showed Napoleon engaged in threesomes, wearing costumes and more. When she got to the last one, thirty-eight photos later, there was a message attached – *Check your email.*

Surely there can't be more than this. What a mess, Maiya thought, shaking her head. Even so, she grabbed her laptop, sat down in a nearby chair, and checked her email.

"Why not? I have nothing more to lose. Everything is gone anyway." She sighed heavily, starkly aware that she was not referring to the stuff that Napoleon took. Maiya felt like she'd lost herself. All she had left was her children.

When she opened her email, she was catapulted into shock again. It was a video this time. The disgusting video featured all types of debauchery, but most of all, betrayal.

"Shut the front door! No, no, no! In my house? In my bed? No!" she said frantically as the video played, revealing Napoleon, Dwayne, and some unknown woman in Maiya's bed. Her bed! The very bed she'd slept in with her husband.

"That's it. Enough is enough!" Anger settled upon her quickly. She grew sick to her stomach. She started reeling although she was still sitting down. The room felt like it was spinning. She closed her eyes and tried to steady herself.

Opening her eyes moments later, she slung the laptop to the floor and jumped up. She immediately searched for her rescue inhaler, but couldn't find it. The dizziness she felt seemed to be getting worse. The rage that she'd been praying to release returned with a vengeance. It had been allowed reentrance into her life from this new round of hurt and pain.

As the need to confront Napoleon overrode her need to find her inhaler, Maiya snatched up her phone and held down the number two. That was the speed dial number to his original phone number. Although, he'd gotten that second phone with a different number, he also kept his original number as well.

"This is the Bishop." As usual, he answered the phone in arrogance.

"Napoleon, what the hell?" Maiya started in on him as soon as he picked up.

"Lady, what is it? I'm umm…busy."

"I saw your pictures," Maiya said, gasping for air. She could feel her chest tightening even more. She started searching for her inhaler again.

No sound came from his end of the line. She didn't even hear him breathing. Had he hung up?

"I saw your filthy videos too…in our house, in our bed. Napoleon, are you crazy? Are you serious?" Maiya flopped back down in the chair and reached for her inhaler when she finally spotted it on the lampstand. She took several puffs of the medicine and several deep breaths.

Napoleon said nothing. Silence was his answer.

At that point, Maiya really didn't need an answer from him. Taking a moment to look at the phone to make sure it was still connected; she put it back to her ear, took another long deep breath and said in a flat tone, "We're getting a divorce."

"Lady, a divorce? Hold up, you can't prove any of that. You ain't got no pictures or videos, so quit lying. I swear you're the biggest liar," Napoleon said, suddenly having lots of things to say as he tried to shift the accusations of wrongdoing to Maiya.

Instead of answering him with words or more bickering, she forwarded him a few pictures via text messages.

"Hold on. Somebody is texting me," Napoleon said, unaware that it was her.

Maiya heard him swear sharply underneath his breath a few seconds later; indicating that he now knew who'd sent those text messages.

"I'll call you back," he said, not sounding so arrogant now.

"Don't bother."

Click.

After hanging up on him, Maiya went back to bed or rather made a pallet on the floor. She couldn't stand the thought of being in that bed. Not now. Truthfully, she just couldn't handle it. All she wanted at that moment was to steady her ragged breathing pattern and go to sleep.

* * * * *

From that day forward, Maiya's self-esteem and confidence plummeted through the floor. She just couldn't seem to wrap her mind around everything that occurred in her life so quickly. She cried out many days, wondering why she hadn't been enough for Napoleon. Why she wasn't enough on multiple levels.

Maiya prayed, often asking the Lord to show her what was wrong with her. She questioned everything about herself, her calling, her anointing, her womanhood – everything.

She constantly chided herself for having missed or dismissed so many things that were right in front of her. Her – the prophet, the preacher, the discerner. She'd been living with a counterfeit worshipper, a false prophet, a fake and she missed it. It made her doubt herself more and more with each passing day.

All Maiya knew was – what she *thought* she knew wasn't what she knew at all. What she thought was a blessed life with a great husband and family were all lies. Unfortunately, that particular revelation consumed her for months.

CHAPTER NINETEEN
Turned Tables

As the weeks turned into months, Maiya continued to allow herself to slip into a place of severe depression. Many days she couldn't explain or express how she felt, so she didn't try. Some days she didn't even feel like living. Her healing occurred at a snail's pace, leaving most of her emotions still tattered and battered.

Maiya was so broken that she eventually stopped going to church. That was extremely unusual for her. She loved the corporate worship experience and actually missed it, but it was just too hard to keep going.

Whatever Maiya turned on to make it through each day, she immediately shut it off when she pulled into the driveway of the house that she still had a mortgage on. There was something depressing about coming home every day to what used to be their home – the house that she'd made into a home with Napoleon.

Once Maiya entered the house, she walked upstairs and went straight to her bedroom. The television stayed on. She didn't watch it though. It just provided some noise and helped to avoid the silence that started to wear on her.

The only time Maiya spent outside of her room was when she talked and fellowshipped with her children. She did her best to make sure life was as normal as possible for them. They were the only reasons she refurnished the downstairs.

As the time neared for Maiya to attend the national conference, she still couldn't shake her depression. She found it increasingly harder to live in that house. It seemed to be draining the life out of her day by day.

When will the pain end, Lord? Maiya prayed, missing who she was before the betrayal as she lay in bed, staring blankly up at the ceiling.

Her alarm clock went off, jerking her from her thoughts and serving as a reminder about today's ministry meeting.

Maiya forced herself out of bed and went to shower. Thankfully the meeting was being held at her house, so she didn't have to be in the public eye any more than necessary. She was even more grateful that the people she was meeting with today were all inner circle folks.

* * * * *

Angie and Van arrived at Maiya's house around the same time. Angie had a spare key, so she let them in. She sent a text to Maiya to let her know that they were there and what room they would be in. She also told her to take her time getting ready. They were in no rush.

Van went to set up their laptops in the renovated family room while Angie went to the kitchen and made herbal tea for the meeting. Today they were going to discuss any remaining conference details and finalize some documents that still needed Maiya's signature.

As Angie was setting up the serving tray on the coffee table, the doorbell rang. She quickly placed a set of blue decorative napkins beside the silver tray, handed Van the energy drink he preferred, and went to answer the front door.

"Hey there, lady," Angie said when she saw who was on the other side of the door.

"Hey, Angie." Star smiled. "I just stopped by to see if Maiya needed anything. How is our girl doing today?"

"She's upstairs getting ready for our meeting right now. Feel free to join us. As for how she's doing, emotionally and spiritually, she's about the same. There hasn't been much of a change in her demeanor," Angie replied, opening the door wider for her to enter.

"Not good," Star said, following her to the family room.

"No, not good at all." Angie frowned.

"Hi, Van," Star said, heading straight for the plush tan and blue sectional when she entered the room. That comfortable piece of furniture had quickly become everyone's favorite place to sit. Maiya ordered it from an online furniture gallery. Despite her current turmoil, her eye for quality had not been compromised by her pain.

"Hi, Star." Van looked up from his work and smiled at her. "How are you?"

"I'm great. Just concerned about Maiya," Star replied.

"Yes, we all are." Angie took her seat by the other laptop to Van's right.

"Okay, y'all. We've got to do something to help her," Star said, looking to Van and Angie. "I know you all are here with her a lot more than I am, but I've never seen her like this before. It's like she's lifeless. She puts up a good front when she's among those who don't really know her, but I see right through that."

"Yeah, I know," Angie said. "I've tried to get her to come to some functions and interact more, but so far all she's been willing to do is have a few meetings. After that, she's right back in this house. She is seriously considering pulling out of the conference with Bishop Horton. She even called to tell him that."

"Why would she do that?" Star looked perplexed.

"She said she doesn't feel worthy or able to minister on that level now," Angie explained.

"Not worthy?" Star sounded confused. "Maiya is *supposed* to be at that conference. There is a word in her that people need. And what did Bishop Horton say? Please don't tell me he accepted her withdrawal."

"I don't know if he accepted her withdrawal or not. All Maiya told me is that he was not judgmental about anything that she shared with him. She said he prayed with her. Then he encouraged her to start her life over and take some time to work on herself," Angie said.

"Okay, that's good. But what about the conference?" Star insisted. "I don't want Maiya to forfeit this divine opportunity."

"I really don't know what Maiya is going to do. But I can tell you this; she is having a hard time moving on. It's not helping at all that Napoleon seems to have some type of personal vendetta against her," Angie said angrily.

"A what? Why in the world would he have a vendetta against her? If anything it should be the other way around." Star shook her head in dismay.

"It seems that Napoleon has called Maiya's pastor and some of the other local pastors and lied about her being gay." Angie spoke in a hushed tone. She didn't want Maiya to walk in and have to hear this all over again. "He also accused her of forcing him out of their home and leaving him with nothing."

"Is that man crazy? Never mind, he's stupid," Star said, answering her own question. "I can only imagine how hurtful that is to Maiya." She shook her head yet again.

"Yeah, well what's worse is the fact that some people actually believe the crap he's spewing!" Angie responded through clenched teeth.

"What about Bishop Horton? Did he buy into that foolishness?" Star asked anxiously.

"I don't know, Star. I don't think he did considering Maiya said that he was encouraging to her. But it still didn't seem to help her. She's really struggling. Sometimes I think she is drowning in her pain. I'm really concerned about what this is doing to her." Angie used a napkin to wipe tears from the corners of her eyes. The tea cups themselves remained untouched in this intense moment. Van had yet to even take a sip of his energy drink.

"Oh, Lord, we've got to do something," Star said.

"We've got to continue to pray, first and foremost," Van interjected finally, after listening intently to them go back and forth. "From the sound of it, Maiya is in a place of unforgiveness and it has a hold on her. I've learned that until we forgive, the pain and the person who inflicted the pain on us will have power over us."

"Of course we will continue to pray, yet it seems that nothing and no one can penetrate those walls that Maiya has erected." More tears welled up in Angie's eyes. "Lord, have mercy. Y'all just don't know how rough her nights are. Maiya is not only hurt, she is enraged. Her words are more negative than I've ever heard coming from her. It seems like she can't even see life *in* herself or *for* herself anymore. And inside this house, when the makeup comes off and there is no one around but the two of us, she frowns continually." Angie dropped her head in her hands and allowed her tears to flow freely.

"I know," Van said flatly. "I've seen her smile during a meeting and even heard her laugh during a conference call, then turn around and frown or cry as soon as they're over. You know how much I love Maiya. She means the world to Janine and me. That's why we now have to pray more strategically. If we truly want to help her, we've got to ask the Lord how to pray more *specifically* in order to get to the root of her issues," he concluded softly.

"I agree, Van." Star nodded. Then she turned to Angie. "Let me ask you something? Has Maiya been singing at all? Even around the house?"

"No. Not one note," Angie replied without lifting her head.

"Not good." Star frowned. "I have never known for Maiya *not* to sing. She always said that music was her refuge."

"Yes, that is what she always told me too." Van nodded. "She even taught me the importance of music in life and how it could usher a person into the very presence of God."

"I suggest we touch and agree now, because we can't let our girl go out like this," Star said, looking like she was ready to take on a legion of devils as she sprung to her feet. "She needs us just as much as we need her."

"I'm ready," Angie said with urgency, standing to her feet as well. "Let's pray right now."

"Me too." Van stood also, his eyes flashing like a warrior's. "And we will pray specifically about that root of unforgiveness that God just revealed."

Angie and Star nodded as they all joined hands.

Van led them in prayer, praising God in advance for Maiya's deliverance as they attacked the spirit of unforgiveness that was coming against her. When he concluded his prayer, Star and Angie prayed respectively. They each prayed for guidance and strength. They asked God to help them pour into Maiya whatever she needed to pull through this ordeal.

* * * * *

Maiya was on her way downstairs when she heard genuine prayers on her behalf. *Wow! My own personal gladiators,* she thought as she stopped and continued to listen to Angie, Van, and Star travailing on her behalf.

She knew they'd been praying for her the whole time, but to actually hear their sincere pleas and intercession did something to her on the inside. It pierced her heart. For the first time in a long while, she felt something other than hurt or anger.

When she heard Angie conclude her prayer, Maiya walked down the stairs and made her way into the family room. When she entered the room, she just looked at each of them with tears in her eyes.

"Thank you all for loving me," she said, dropping her head and letting her tears fall freely. They rushed over and hugged her. They spoke words of affirmation and encouragement to her until her tears subsided.

"Okay, y'all. It's time for me to share some things," Maiya said once they were settled down on the sectional with their respective beverages in hand. "Some *bad* things," she added in order to prepare them for the worst.

"There's more?" Star lifted her left eyebrow and put her cup down on the coffee table. Angie and Van followed suit with their beverages.

"Yes, *much* more," Maiya replied, putting her cup down as well. "First, I have to say thank you again. I know it's been hard watching all of this unfold and not really knowing what was going to happen. I could not have asked God for better family and friends."

"No thanks necessary, My," Van assured her. "This is what we do."

"Exactly!" Angie chimed in. "We wouldn't have it any other way."

"What they said!" Star pointed the index fingers of both hands to Angie and Van. They all laughed at her animated response.

"Well, I appreciate you and I wanted to make sure I told you that. I don't take you all for granted." Maiya paused and sighed. "There are so many things that have happened. I don't even know where to start." She shrugged.

"Just start wherever you feel comfortable." Star reached over and soothingly rubbed her arm.

"Well, I'm sure you all have noticed that I've been pretty quiet lately," Maiya said seriously. "It's been a rough time and I'm just unsure about a lot of things right now. Worst of all, I feel so ashamed. Whew!" she said, shaking her head. "I didn't think I'd ever be able to say that last part out loud. But it's true. I do feel ashamed."

"Maiya, you have nothing to be ashamed of." Star reached for her left hand.

"I hear you, Star, but I missed so much and I dismissed even more. I don't even know which is which at this point. I just feel like everything has come crashing down around me and that maybe I wasn't supposed to do any of this." Maiya shrugged again.

"We can't pretend to understand what you're going through or how you feel, but we do know that you can make it through this. You're Maiya Jackson and as you always tell us, everything you need is in you," Angie said with great conviction.

"I don't know, y'all. It just seems like it's taking me forever to move beyond this and it's all so overwhelming. Y'all don't even know the half of it," Maiya said.

"My, we really don't have to know the details. You know it's not necessary to tell us. What we do know is that the God in you would not give up on us, so we're not about to give up on you," Van said very firmly. "Angie told us about you wanting to pull out of the conference and I do not agree with that. Not one bit."

"I knew you wouldn't," Maiya responded flatly. "I just don't know what else to do right now. I guess I should tell you all that I'm also considering dismantling the ministry. I'm not sure that I can handle it anymore. I can't focus and this pretending to get through isn't working." She looked at them directly. "Of course I'll make sure that y'all are taken care of. I wouldn't have it any other way," she reassured them.

"Oh no, ma'am," Star spoke up in a very sharp tone. "Now I know you're hurting, but what you're not going to do is let some fool make you bow out of what God has done for you. Chamaiya LaShelle Jackson, you are *not* a quitter. Regardless of how you feel, you have to remember what and who you know. Now I know exactly where you came from and what you came through and baby girl, just like God delivered you then, He's going to do it again. There will be no shutting down anything. I'm calling Mama right now. And I'm not talking about Nicole either since I know you two still don't see eye to eye," Star clarified, pulling out her black cell phone.

"No wait, Star! You don't have to call Mama Ludie." Maiya held up both hands. "I don't want her worrying even more than she already has. She has been incredible to me and the kids, especially since granny passed, so please don't call her. Just hear me out please and I think y'all will understand why I feel like this."

"Okay, out with it," Star said, returning her cell phone to its resting place.

Maiya nodded. It was time to reveal all. She was done covering for someone who obviously never covered her.

CHAPTER TWENTY
The Ugly Truth

Maiya could almost hear a pin drop in the room as Angie, Star, and Van sat with anxious eyes, yet patiently waiting for her to share the rest of her heart. They prayed in the Spirit beneath their breaths, outwardly maintaining a posture of prayer concerning her.

Maiya took a deep breath and then released the ugly truth that she'd been too ashamed to expose before. "I don't know which direction my life is going in right now and this is partly why. First, Napoleon has wiped out both of my personal accounts. Secondly, and this is what I'm more concerned about, I found out that Napoleon hasn't just been cheating with women. He's been sleeping with men, too. Well, there is at least one that I definitely know about."

"What!" they yelled in unison.

Van jumped up from his seat and started pacing the floor.

Angie dropped her head.

Star's eyes bulged from her head.

"Yeah, that's what I said too, along with some other things once the initial shock wore off," Maiya continued. "That meant I had to go back to the doctor and get even more extensive tests done, especially after he gave me that STD. So far the results have been negative for any other diseases. I have to be tested every three months for the next year for HIV. Every time I walk into that office for those appointments and think of why I have to be there, I'm slammed with an influx of fear and hurt all over again."

"Hold on, Maiya. Don't start thinking the worst," Van said, turning to look at her. "We have to continue believing God for more good reports."

"I don't know what to think, Van," Maiya said softly. Tears fell from her eyes again. "Right now my emotions and thoughts are so sporadic.

Sometimes I'm up and sometimes I'm down. Some days I receive all the good that is coming my way. Other days absolutely nothing penetrates me. The sad part is that I realize it, but I don't know how to pull myself out. I feel like I'm in an internal tug-of-war."

"Oh my God!" Tears welled up in Star's eyes. "Maiya, I'm so sorry that you've experienced all this." She blinked her eyes clear as a determined look settled upon her face. "I will be going to the remaining doctor's appointments with you. No arguments. I'm going!" she said firmly.

"And you know I'm taking care of the ministry business, so don't worry about that," Angie inserted just as firmly. "I have rerouted your ministry calls for now. I also terminated Allysa and to her credit, she went quietly into the night." She briefly paused and added, "Oh, and the household bills are taken care of."

"I have no arguments concerning the calls or Allysa, but as for the household bills…" Maiya's words trailed off as she looked at Angie with a raised brow.

"Well, I have to confess that we already knew about Napoleon wiping out your bank accounts," Angie responded softly. There was no need to say anything further about Allysa. That chapter was closed. "The bank called me when they couldn't reach you since I'm listed as an additional contact for urgent matters," she explained. "When they told me that someone, who was not authorized, tried to access our business accounts, I had them check your personal accounts as well."

"Okay. But how did you pay my household bills, Angie?" Maiya asked, now understanding why she hadn't been hounded by her creditors lately. "I haven't gotten any of that money back for those accounts and it doesn't look like I ever will."

"I took care of it. Don't worry about how," Angie said very sternly.

"Well, all right then." Maiya sighed, sat back on the couch and covered her face with her hands. She didn't have the energy to go back and forth with Angie. It was taking everything in her just to have this conversation. She didn't know whether to cry because Angie had taken care of the bills or to cry because she was embarrassed that she couldn't take care of them herself.

"Thank you," Maiya finally said in a humble tone as she uncovered her face.

"Well, this is what I know," Van said, finally rejoining the conversation as he took his seat again. "Either Janine and I are staying here with you and the kids or y'all are coming home with us. Those are your choices, unless you want to go with Star or Angie, but you're *not* staying alone. Not anymore. We're not going to go wondering if you're okay or just seeing you briefly when we bring meals over for you and the kids. Or in Star and Angie's case, spending the occasional nights here. From now on, we are going to *know* that you're well every second of the day and night." Every word he spoke was with authority.

"I'm fine. Y'all don't have to do all that," Maiya objected. "You've done enough as it is and you've been so great with the kids. They almost live with y'all now," she said half-jokingly. "No telling when Janine will be bringing them back today."

No one said a word in response. They looked at her like she'd grown a third eye in the middle of her forehead. Their knowing expressions were enough to convince Maiya that they were not buying her 'I'm fine' bit. Yet she refused to let it go.

"What?" Maiya looked around at her three friends. "I'm really okay. Really."

Star stood up and grabbed Maiya by the hand. She walked her over to the long mirrored wall in the family room. "Look! You know I love you, but, boo, you look a hot mess and I'm not just talking about your physical appearance either. Look at you. *That's* not Maiya." She pointed to the mirror.

"Yes, it is." Maiya slightly shrugged as she looked at her reflection.

"Really now?" Star stood with her hands on her tiny waist. "Maiya, let's be honest. Your hair has never had that many split ends, not even in college when we couldn't afford a stylist. And when did you start biting your nails again? That alone proves to me that your nerves are surely shot. That cute designer sweat suit that you love so much is hanging off of you. Your face is extremely thin, which indicates that you are not eating properly. And those dark circles around your eyes tell me that you are not sleeping properly either. Baby girl, you are a lot of things but okay, fine, or good, you are not. You don't have to pretend around us because we love you. We don't care if you're not okay right now. We just want to help you be okay eventually."

"It's Maiya. She's just broken," she said, referring to herself in the third person. "All of those reasons that you just stated, are why I'm going to call Bishop Horton and officially take my name out of the lineup for the conference. I thought I was ready, but this has proven to me that I'm not." She took her seat on the sectional again and dropped her head.

In her peripheral vision, Maiya could see tears swimming in Angie's eyes. She looked like she didn't know what to say to her, so she just grabbed Maiya's right hand and held it. That simple gesture brought some much needed comfort.

"Maiya, I have something to tell you," Van spoke again.

"What's that?" Maiya lifted her head and looked at him.

"You can't withdraw from that line up. You are meant to be at that particular conference—"

"Van, I know what you're trying to do, but it's not necessary. It's just not time yet. It may never be," Maiya objected quickly.

"Maiya, have you forgotten what you will be ministering about?" Van got up and started pacing the floor again. He did that whenever God was giving him a Rhema word. "It's Restoration! Can't you see that God allowed you to go through all of that, so you'll be more effective when you minister this to others? You had to go through this even though it doesn't seem fair and you appear to be the one who is losing." He stopped pacing and turned to face her directly. "Maiya, you're not losing. You're winning. Because when God restores you, He's going to make you *better* than you were before. You won't be the same Maiya. You won't feel the same or think the same. Please don't let the enemy steal your restoration from you."

"But..." Maiya began.

"But nothing," Van interrupted. "Or rather 'But God'! That's the only 'but' that we get to have in this walk. Do you remember what you told me months ago? You're called to this. You're more than capable to do this. Everything you need is in you to do this. I think everyone in this room will agree that you should be the one doing this conference."

Star, Angie and Van laughed. They were tickled by how he'd turned Maiya's words on her. Yet he meant them wholeheartedly.

Maiya laughed too. It had been so long since she genuinely laughed like this. Too long.

"Maiya, I have to agree with Van," Star said, turning serious again. "You have to go. There's something special *in* you and *about* you. Something special that people need to see. I believe that's why God allowed *you* to go through this and not someone else. Not everyone could handle the trauma that you've experienced in your life and victoriously lived to tell about it. You're not a victim, you're not a sob story, and you're not a quitter! Oh hallelujah!" she continued, sounding more excited and inspired by the moment.

"Praise the Lord!" Angie said, looking equally inspired and excited.

"Whether you want to hear it or not, God has allowed these things in your life because He can trust you to stay in the race." Star jumped up from her seat and moved to stand directly in front of Maiya. "I know you've had some bumps, bruises, cuts and wounds, but you're a soldier. You're different, Maiya, and it's evident."

Maiya dropped her head yet again. She heard Star loud and clear. She just didn't know how to make her understand that even with all that Star thought she possessed, she still felt destitute. She didn't see those things in herself. Not anymore.

Star kneeled down in front of her. "You really can withstand the fiery darts of the enemy. Maiya, you are equipped!" she encouraged, lifting her chin up with one finger. "It's time to lift your head back up."

"My story is no different from any other woman or person for that matter who has been through abuse, abandonment, neglect, depression or any of these things." Maiya shrugged.

"I didn't say your story was different, I said *you* are different. How you end will be different," Star said, rising to her feet again. "This was definitely an attack of the enemy, but I must remind you that what the enemy tried to use for bad, God will turn it around and use it for your good. There is a standard that God has lifted on your behalf. It may be flooding, but you are not drowning!" She pointed that skinny finger at Maiya as only she could.

"I know that's right, Star! Say that!" Angie piped in. "Maiya, we're here because we love you and because we believe in you and who you are in God. Don't think for a second that we have counted you out and neither has God. More than ever, we believe that the greatness in you is about to rise up stronger than ever. Your mind and thoughts may be raging right now, but God has kept you through all of this. He will continue to keep you."

Maiya's brows rose as Angie jumped up from the couch and started walking around the room like Van and Star were doing. *Lord, help me to help them understand that I just can't right now. It's too much. I don't even know whether I'm coming or going sometimes*, she prayed as she listened to her friends.

"You're going to that conference and you are going – restored," Angie declared. "The next time you open your mouth to speak, hell is going to have a hard time and Heaven is going to be pouring out the overflow. You're hurting right now, but the way you're about to annihilate the enemy, girl, I can't wait to see that!"

Angie, Star and Van slapped each other high-five in passing. The trio continued to pace the floor, giving praise to God.

"Well, I'm glad you all have so much confidence in me," Maiya said weakly, wishing she had more confidence in herself. "I hear what you all are saying. I just don't see it happening."

"Maiya, our confidence is in the God that's in you and that's where you're going to have to pull yours from," Van said pointedly. "You've always said you can't do it without Him. Well, you can definitely do it *with* Him. Oh, that's good right there." He clapped his hands.

"It's apparent that I can't argue or win with you three, but I do love you for loving me," Maiya said. "I just don't know what to think right now. So much has happened so quickly. I do know one thing though." She paused in deep thought.

"What?" they asked in unison when her silence lingered beyond five seconds.

"I'm selling this house. If I could give it away, I would," Maiya stated firmly. "That's one thing I'm not indecisive about. Van, please tell Janine that I want the house on the market immediately. I'm confident that her company can sell this property quickly."

"Ah, where are you going in the meantime?" Star inquired.

"I don't know," Maiya replied, "but it won't be here."

"Isn't the house in both of your names?" Van asked hesitantly.

"No. It's only in *my* name. *Everything* is in my name," Maiya explained. "As a matter of fact, hold up one minute. I have a Cadillac that's still in my name too. A Cadillac to repossess right now," she said, looking for her cell phone. It was on a nearby end table beside her iPad.

The trio's eyes were wide with shock. Even Angie didn't know that bit of information.

"Who are you calling?" Star asked.

"Tony. He'll have it back in my garage in a few hours," Maiya said, scrolling through her phone for his number. The iPad was now in her lap.

"Do you mean Tony Blackwell that you went to school with?" Star asked.

"Yep, the one I used to sing with. One call and he will be on it," Maiya replied.

"Tony is a good guy and he still loves you dearly," Van shared. "We've been the best of friends for many years."

"Yes, he's a very good guy. Although he's loved me since forever, he's never disrespected any of my marriages and he has kept his promise to always be there for me," Maiya said right before Tony answered the phone.

"Hey, beautiful," Tony said, greeting her the same way he had for twenty-five years.

"Hey, Tony. I need a favor," Maiya said quickly.

"What's up? Anything for you," he replied genuinely.

"I need you to locate and pick up the black Cadillac that Napoleon drives. It has a security feature on it that will locate it if it's stolen. I will activate it from my iPad, so you can find it," Maiya said, doing just that as she spoke.

"Somebody stole the car? That's messed up," Tony said, making the most logical assumption. "Okay, pretty lady. I'm pulling up my system right now."

"No. Napoleon just isn't the driver of it anymore. I'm going to sell it once you get it back to me," Maiya explained.

"Are you all right?" Tony asked with concern in his voice. "I don't like the sound of this. Did he do something to you? If he has, let me know and I'll take care of that too," he said, sounding as protective as ever of her.

"We've been friends too long for me to lie to you. I just don't want to talk about it right now. It's too much and it would take too long. I just need you to do this one favor for me." Maiya didn't want to involve him in this mess more than necessary.

"Consider it done," Tony said, typing so loud that she could hear his fingers flying over the keys. "I have located the car. I'm headed to get it now. I'll see you soon." He paused and added with even more concern, "Um...Maiya, are you alone? I really don't think you should be alone right now."

"No. Van, Angie, and Star are here." Maiya smiled at them. "I'm blessed to have them in my corner."

"Okay, good." Tony sounded relieved. "See you later," he concluded and then ended the call.

CHAPTER TWENTY-ONE
Prayer Still Works

As another week passed, Maiya remained very selective in her interaction with others. Although her conversation was still limited, she was slowly coming out of depression. Fortunately, she started earnestly praying again since that day of prayer with her friends. She was also sleeping better. Naps had become one of her best friends.

Maiya was awakened from today's late afternoon nap by loud voices coming from downstairs. Those voices sounded friendly so she took her time stretching and getting up from the purple chaise lounge she'd slept on.

Following the noise to its source, Maiya ended up in the family room. She was surprised to see that her whole team was there. Van, Angie, Maria, Jasmine, Vickie, and Kymberli – they were all there. The floor and the sectional were covered with these beautiful people that loved her and had remained faithful to her.

Lying on the floor and lounging on the sectional was customary for them whenever they hung out at her house. They sounded like a group of teenagers, laughing at the top of their voices. When they saw Maiya walk in, they burst out laughing again.

"What is so funny? And what are all y'all doing here?" Maiya asked, watching them topple over one another, laughing hysterically. "By the way, what time is it?" She stretched some more and willed herself to wake up fully. That was the best she'd slept in a very long time. "And what day is it?" She rubbed her eyes and shook her head quickly from side to side.

They laughed even louder at those questions, which she hadn't given them a chance to answer in her sleepy ramblings.

"Maiya, we're laughing because we said you were going to be delusional when you finally woke up," Angie finally responded through her laughter.

"Girl, you've been sleep for a whole day."

"A *whole* day? You have got to be kidding me. Did y'all give me something?" Maiya asked, feeling bewildered and no doubt looking the same way.

They laughed even harder.

Maiya finally smiled. She felt a sense of calm and peace being with them. Both of those feelings had been missing from her life lately.

Welcome back, she thought, loving the emotional place she was currently in. *Wait a minute...have I really been asleep for a whole day? Then that means...*Her thoughts halted as realization set in.

Suddenly she turned around and sprinted from the room.

"Maiya, where are you going?" Van yelled behind her.

"If I've been sleep for a whole day, then I'm *long* overdue for a shower," she yelled over her left shoulder. "Be right back."

More laughter ensued behind her.

* * * * *

"Now who is going to tell her why we are *really* here?" Jasmine asked, looking to Angie and Van for the answer after Maiya left the room. "And just how do y'all plan on getting her to go to church with us tonight?"

"Oh, she's going tonight," Van said in a serious tone.

"How do you know that?" Angie asked. "Do you know something that we don't?"

"God said it!" Van replied firmly and yet calmly with a shrug. "He said it's time for her to break free of this internal prison that she's in. There is a word from God for her tonight. That's also why I called you all here. She's going to need our support tonight. *All* of us." He pointed around the room at each person.

"But *how* do you plan on getting her to go?" Maria asked. She was usually their most quiet team member. Yet when she spoke, it always packed a huge punch.

"I've worked with Maiya just about as long as you all have and so I know she can be very stubborn at times," Maria continued. "As a matter of fact, that's how I ended up on the team, remember? She was relentless. She kept saying God told me you are supposed to be on this team and she didn't back down. She didn't force me, but every time she saw me and every time I called her, she would remind me of what God said."

"Yeah. I remember the final time Maiya told you that," Angie said. "Girl, the look on your face when she called you up to the front of that church was priceless. Oh my goodness, where were we that day?"

"North Carolina!" Maria blurted out with a loud laugh. "I will never forget it," she said through more laughter. "I was trying to hide from her. I knew she was going to get me. I felt it as soon as I walked in the building." She ducked like she had on the day of that encounter.

The group laughed as she illustrated her attempt to hide from Maiya.

"Y'all are laughing, but I clearly remember saying on that day, I'm sitting in the back, because I'm not fooling around with Maiya Jackson today," Maria continued.

They howled in laughter.

"Ha! You thought you were going to be able to hide from her. Better yet, you thought you were going to hide from God!" Angie laughed so hard she had tears in her eyes. She bent over and hugged her mid-section to keep her sides from hurting.

"Girl, I know. But I tried it," Maria said, taking on a serious tone. "Truthfully y'all, Maiya was absolutely right. I knew it was straight from God, because she called out what I hid the most – my fear. Then she spoke life into me and prayed that I would not keep allowing fear to hold me back. My life truly changed for the better when I obeyed God. I really loved the day-to-day operations of a business, but I was equally afraid that I couldn't do this job. I feared that it was too big for me to handle and especially in a ministry. But every word that God said through that woman has manifested and then some."

Van jumped up from his seat and started pacing the floor, almost at a run. "That's exactly it!" he semi-shouted, turning to look at them with wide eyes. "Maria, if God told Maiya something for you and it happened, then I believe that what He told me concerning her is going to happen too. Tonight!"

Van began to pace faster. "I'm not going to relent and neither are you all. I have learned that there are some things that you can't worry about how they are going to happen. You just have to believe that they will happen because God said it!"

"Well, I believe she's going to go," Angie said decisively. "We should all be standing in agreement with that."

"Amen," the team responded in unison.

"Amen? What is everyone saying amen to?" Maiya asked, walking back into the room. She'd pulled her tree braids up into a ponytail and was wearing her favorite purple and white jogging suit with matching running shoes.

Everyone in the room grew quiet.

"Ah hello, people? Amen what?" Maiya asked again.

Van was the first to speak up. "Oh, we're all going to church together tonight." He smiled from ear to ear.

"Oh okay. Well, I'm sure it's going to be a good service. It's great that you all are going together," Maiya said. "What's the occasion?"

"Maiya," Van said, calling her name softly.

"Yes?"

"We are *all* going, including *you*," he said firmly, crossing his arms across his chest as an added measure.

"I see. So that's what all of you are doing here?" Maiya looked around the room. "That's funny."

Van suddenly started praying, catching her completely off guard. "Father God, in Jesus Name, we thank You that You are not a man that You should lie, neither the son of man that You should repent. Lord, we thank You that Your Word will not return void and that it will accomplish what You sent it to do."

Maiya stood in silent shock, watching as each team member rose and joined hands while Van continued to pray.

Angie held her hand out to her and would not take no for an answer.

Maiya finally joined the circle and bowed her head. She listened as they prayed and cried out to the Lord on her behalf.

"Father we don't want our will done. Our desire is for Your will to be done in our lives," Van continued. "In Jesus Name, Lord, send Your anointing to destroy every yoke of bondage, break down every barrier and wipe out every obstacle. Father, we plead the blood of Jesus over Maiya. God, we believe that You will restore her. We thank You in advance that You are reviving and renewing everything about her.

Father, we ask You to give back to her everything that the enemy has taken. We bind up the spirit of depression in the name of Jesus. We come against low self-esteem in Jesus Name. We plead the blood of Jesus against every demonic attack. Satan, you have no power over Maiya. Jesus, You have all power. You reign over everything. Reign in her life now, Jesus. Reign in her mind, Jesus. Reign in her heart, Jesus. Take control. Drive out every hurt, every emotion, and every spirit that's not like You. We need You to flood her with Your love, Lord, like never before and we thank You and praise You because it is so. In Jesus Name. Amen," Van concluded.

As everyone uttered, "Amen", Jasmine started praying. Each one prayed, one after the other non-stop, becoming a true prayer circle. Tears streamed down their faces. By the time they reached Angie, who was the last to pray, Maiya was crying uncontrollably and clapping her hands.

"Hallelujah," Maiya cried out weakly. "Thank You, Jesus." She clapped slowly as she praised God. She could feel the presence of the Lord getting stronger and stronger in the room. "Help me, Lord. Please help me, Lord," she prayed, feeling her body go limp.

Van grabbed Maiya and held her up.

"God, I'm ready to give it all up. I've worked so hard, Lord, to do what You wanted and my life is in shambles. Please, Jesus, help me. I don't know what else to say to You, Lord, but please help me. My heart is so broken, Lord. I failed, Lord. Nobody don't want me," Maiya said, pouring out the raw contents of her heavy heart, uncaring if they were politically or grammatically correct.

Van held on to her tighter.

"Why, Lord? Why they don't want me? Everybody always leaves and it's worse now, God. Please, God, please. I want somebody to love me. Please, God. Just one time," Maiya continued. "What's wrong with me? I tried so hard, God. I was so good to that man. I loved him. Please, God, please help me. God, I'm sorry if I did something wrong, but please don't leave me like this. I can't live...I can't live like this no more, Lord. Please, I'm begging You, God, please. God, it hurts so bad. I didn't do nothing to him. Jesus, please! Jesus!" Her voice raised another octave with each new heartrending statement until she was literally screaming the Lord's name at the end.

Spent, Maiya crumpled to the floor, inadvertently pulling Van down with her as the anointing upon her grew heavier than her pain. "Jesus, please help me. Lord, have mercy. Please Jesus," she said repetitively, holding on to that powerful Name with everything she had in her.

Everyone gathered around Maiya on the floor. They sat with her in silence as she sobbed even more uncontrollably. They hugged one another. Each one laid hands on her at some point and continued to pray silently.

An hour and a half later, they were still sitting on the floor. All eyes were dry as Maiya rested her head upon Angie's right shoulder.

"You are my hiding place," Maiya sang as she closed her eyes. "My strength when I am weak, my joy when I'm sad, my laughter when I'm mad. You are my hiding place."

Jasmine and Van began to sing along with her.

"In You, I live. In You, I move. In You, I have my being. You are my hiding place. Can't live without You. Can't move without You. I can't be without You. My hiding place. You are my hiding..." Maiya's voice trailed off.

They continued to sing the rest of the song for her. It ministered to Maiya in a new way. Now she knew why God had her to write that song so long ago.

"I'm going to get dressed," Maiya said, getting up from the floor when the song was over.

"No, Maiya," Van said quickly. "It's casual night. You can go as is. We'll be right on time, if we leave now."

"But I..." Maiya touched her bare face.

"I'll give you some makeup in the car, so quit looking like that," Angie said, rising to her feet as well.

They all burst out in laughter again.

"Come on, y'all. We're *all* going to church," Angie concluded with finality.

"Thank You, Jesus!" Van said as they grabbed their belongings and headed out the door.

CHAPTER TWENTY-TWO
Prison Break

While Maiya sat upfront, Angie settled into one of the backseats of Van's new SUV. He just bought the black on black 2014 Cadillac Escalade. From the look of things, it promised to be a luxurious ride for everyone tonight.

Van's new vehicle was a byproduct of his decision to move forward in his career as a motivational speaker. An increase in speaking engagements had shifted his life tremendously, especially financially, which had been a true blessing to his family in so many areas.

As they exited Maiya's driveway, Angie pulled out her phone and sent a text message to Star. The text read: *I apologize for the short notice, but can you and Mama Ludie meet us tonight at church? Maiya is coming with us.*

Star immediately texted back: *YES! What time and where?*

Angie smiled. She quickly texted the address and told her that they were on the way there now.

Mama is already with me, so we will head on over to the church now as well, was Star's reply.

Angie outright grinned now. *God is so good!*

"What are you cheesing so wide about?" Maiya asked, half-turned in her seat.

"Just thinking about how good God is," Angie replied, glad to know that Maiya's spiritual antennas were working fine again. Why else would she pick that particular moment to turn around in her seat?

"Yes, He is," Maiya said, giving her an I-know-there's-more-to-it-than-that look before facing forward again.

* * * * *

Forty-five minutes later, Maiya and her team pulled into the parking lot

113

of the church. She quickly recognized where they were. It was the annual tag team service that was held every year by her former Pastor and his older brother, Bishop Caleb Martin. Both churches came together for this fellowship and she had not missed a service since the year they began. She'd forgotten about it this year...until now.

"Oh, y'all really think y'all slick, don't you?" Maiya said rhetorically with a light chuckle.

"What?" Angie and Van said in unison, trying to look innocent.

Everyone laughed.

"All right, I'm going to let y'all have this one. Y'all got me this time," Maiya said. "I'm here now, but I am not singing, speaking, or nothing else. Does Apostle Martin know that I'm coming?" She lifted her right eyebrow at Angie and Van.

"Nope, I didn't tell anyone. I know how much you love this service, so I decided that we were going to bring you. Well, I decided after God told me, but you know what I mean," Van said, laughing.

"Yeah, yeah, yeah!" Maiya shook her head. "Blame it on the Lawd!"

They all laughed as they climbed out of Van's vehicle.

Maiya stopped suddenly as they approached the door of the church. Those walking behind her almost tripped over one another. They grabbed each other to keep from falling.

"Hold on," Maiya told the group, ready to explain her sudden pause. "I don't want to walk in while they are singing *Cover Me*. I'm telling y'all, I know Apostle Martin. He's going to want me to sing. Can we wait to go in?"

"Nope." Angie quickly grabbed Maiya's hand and literally slung her through the door.

Everyone stifled their laughter as they piled in behind them.

Van entered last, making sure everyone was in safely.

"Let's sit back here please," Maiya pleaded with them as soon as they entered the rear of the church. Even though they entered quickly, her eyes caught sight of the lady in all blue, trembling with her hands lifted. She stood on the far right side of the room next to the man seated with his head bowed. He looked like he was pounding his right fist into his left hand.

Maiya and her team finally stopped five rows from the back. There were enough seats to accommodate everyone. She deliberately took her seat quickly and sat with her head down. She wanted to blend into the congregation, hear the Word and leave.

Ohhhh...I'm gonna get them for this one, Maiya thought right before a jolt of electricity shook her body. She felt a quickening within. Her spirit seemed extremely sensitive for some reason as it picked up more than she thought she'd be able to, especially now.

When the song finally ended, Maiya heard one of the Pastors start the opening remarks. Someone on her right gently touched her hand. She lifted her head and looked at the person. It was Mama Ludie.

"Mama!" Maiya almost screamed. She wrapped her arms around her, hugging her for the longest time.

Angie smiled wide from the seat next to Mama Ludie. That was indication enough for Maiya to know she'd been set up even further tonight.

Maiya was at ease with the familiar calming spirits around her. Before she could turn to look around even more, she felt a light tap on her left shoulder. Looking for the source of that tap, she turned her head slightly to the left. Her eyes immediately welled up with tears as they lit upon Star, who was there tonight too.

Oh they set me up real good, Maiya mused. She hugged Star just as fervently as she had Mama Ludie.

Up and down their row, the whole team wore big, cheesy, kid-like grins.

Maiya couldn't help but smile too. Her tears continued to flow. If she didn't know anything else, she knew that she was surrounded by love right now.

Maiya was also happy to see that Cameron was in attendance as well. She spotted him at the front of the sanctuary. He appeared to be serving as Bishop Martin's armor bearer that night.

As the message started, they all settled into their seats and turned their attention to the pulpit.

Lord, please speak to me tonight, Maiya prayed silently with a spirit of expectancy. *Something is going on within me and I need to know what it is. I need a Word that can only come from You. God, help me cipher through these things I'm picking up in my spirit. I'm feeling overwhelmed right now. It's like something new has opened up in me, but I need You to guide me through whatever this is. Lord Jesus, have mercy!*

Just as Maiya tuned in completely, Apostle Martin said, "Tonight's message is – Prison Break. Beloved, you need to be free from them *and* from you. It's time that you come out of this prison of hurt, pain, and isolation. You are called to this, but you can't do what God called you to do *like* this."

Maiya jerked her head slightly to the left and then to the right, checking for any sign that her inner circle was hearing and receiving the same thing she was. *Did they tell him?* she wondered for a moment, but quickly dismissed that thought. This remnant of people wouldn't have released anything that significant without her consent.

"The enemy has attempted to destroy your confidence and to take everything that you thought was secure from you, but tonight is your night," Apostle Martin continued excitedly. "Tonight is the night of your prison break. Everything that thought it was holding you is about to loose you."

Although he hadn't looked her way, Maiya felt like Apostle Martin was talking directly to her. She stood to her feet instantly as his message hit home.

Many others stood as well. Quite a few people raised their hands in praise and agreement. Resounding "Amens" could be heard from the front to the back of the sanctuary.

"Oh glory!" Maiya shouted, clapping her hands fervently. That declaration made her feel like fire had just been ignited in her spirit. As she lowered her hands, she caught a glimpse of the lady in blue again. She also noticed the menacing look on the man's face right next to her.

My God – she's terrified, Maiya thought when revelation knowledge settled into her spirit. *She's not trembling in the spirit. She's afraid of him. Dear Jesus, have mercy.*

Maiya couldn't shake the image that she saw of the man and woman across the room. But she also knew that she needed God to do something in *her* tonight. She wasn't ready to offer them anything until God gave her something. That something was the power of God for her own life.

Maiya was also acutely aware that it was important to move in His timing. She never wanted to minister out of her pain. She knew the dangers of doing that, so she listened more intently with her spirit from that point on. She blocked out everything and everyone around her. She felt like her life was dependent upon her breaking free tonight. She couldn't minister freedom while living in bondage.

As the tag team message continued, both Pastors declared that internal prison doors were opening in the lives of the people on that night. They spoke about the unfortunate fact that some people experienced bondage at the hands of others and sometimes because of the actions of others.

Bishop Caleb Martin said, "You had to experience this place of bondage and this level of devastation. While you were doing God's will, sons and daughters, it was necessary for you to know what the bound people were going through. Now, because *you've* been through, you're qualified to bring *them* out."

Maiya jumped up and down in front of her seat. The lady in the blue dress walked to the front of the room and stood with her head bowed. Her whole body continued to tremble. Women from the host church instantly surrounded her.

"Amen!" was shouted from all corners of the building again.

Apostle Martin spoke once more, moving the tag team service along at lightning speed. A few times he and his brother actually threw the microphone back and forth across the pulpit to one another.

Apostle Martin walked out of the pulpit as he continued sharing with the people. His stride seemed a little apprehensive as he walked down the right aisle all the way to the back. He looked like he was searching for something or rather someone. He even slowed down the pace of his speech during this part of his message.

Maiya picked up on all of that immediately.

"Beloved, because you know what it's like to be locked up in your emotions and your brokenness, you are qualified to speak freedom in the lives of others," Apostle Martin said, slowly strolling up the center aisle. When he finally stopped, he was one row behind where Maiya stood.

"Now that you know what it's like to be locked up in your mind and in your spirit, God wants to use you to free someone else. He wants to use you as an agent of deliverance. You are a chosen spokesperson for the redemption offered by Christ!" Apostle Martin continued, glancing to the left and the right of him at the standing congregation.

People clapped all around the room.

"Oh, come on now," Apostle Martin said, looking and sounding inspired by his own message. "I hear the Spirit of the Lord saying, come out of that place in Jesus Name! What's in you is not dead. Your life is not over. When you come out this time, you're bringing some other folks out with you." He turned around in circles, swinging his arms.

Suddenly he jumped up in the chair on the end of the row. "Who am I talking to tonight?" Apostle Martin looked around him anxiously. "Your anointing is great and it cannot be killed by what's been done to you. I have a message for you. Hey, God! I hear You, Lord," he shouted emphatically.

By this time, Maiya had moved into the aisle on the far left side of the building. This was not uncommon for her. She usually stood in a place where she could move around freely.

With her hands lifted up and her face turned to the wall, Maiya wailed. Wailed!

"Let me get to her. It's for her!" Apostle Martin shouted as he shot across the room. People scattered when he ran across the chairs.

Blame his urgency on Maiya's shrill cry. It was that cry that lunged Apostle Martin in her direction. When he finally made it over to her and turned her around, his eyes grew big and round in shock, bulging in their sockets.

"Prophetess, it's you! Dear Jesus!" Apostle Martin immediately started speaking life into her in an urgent tone. "My God! Daughter, the Lord said, you are not what they did to you. You are *what* God called you to be. You are *who* God called you to be. In the Name of Jesus, come out this instant! This can't hold you any longer!"

Angie, Van, Star, Maria, and Jasmine were also nearby. When Apostle Martin took off running toward Maiya, they had too. They were in position, praying for her and listening to what the Pastor declared over her life. Mama Ludie knelt on the floor, praying fervently at her chair. Kymberli and Vickie were praying just as fervently at their seats.

"I need everyone in this building to start praying. The devil ought to be ashamed. Oh, but we're about to destroy this tactic in Jesus Name!" Apostle Martin looked intently at Maiya. "Daughter, I have another message for you from God."

Maiya lifted her hands weakly. She felt faint, but her spirit was open and ready to receive.

Angie and Van immediately grabbed her arms. The rest of them moved to stand behind her to make sure her leaning frame didn't fall backward.

"Maiya, the Lord said to tell you that He loves you. He said He heard your prayer and He wants you to know that He loves you *so* much," Apostle Martin prophesied.

Maiya inhaled sharply as something sparked within her. Instantaneously, strength poured into her and she took off running.

Maiya ran around the entire building. That weak, faint feeling had dissipated at those Rhema words. Now she felt like fire blazed up into her body from her feet. She jumped up and down like she was stomping on burning grass. Her arms and hands shook rapidly. Deliverance was taking place.

Her family and loved ones cried, shouted, and praised God. They lifted their hands. Some of them ran along with Maiya.

Mama Ludie stood to her feet now too. Like a loving mother to her child, she kept a watchful eye on Maiya as she worshipped.

Apostle Martin ran behind Maiya through the sanctuary, continuing to speak over her life. The more he declared God's Word over her, the better she felt.

"Hey!" Maiya yelled. "Thank You, Jesus. Thank You, Lord." She spun around in circles. She waved her arms uncontrollably when she finally stopped running and spinning.

"Thank Ya, God! Thank Ya!" Maiya continued in unrestricted and uninhibited praise. Then she went into a praise dance like only she could. Her feet moved extra fast. Her arms mimicked those of a boxer's and her ponytail was long gone. Her face was completely covered by her long strands of hair.

Maiya's praise had a domino effect. It looked like a marathon had begun in the room. Every corner was filled with people shouting praises. Every person was on their feet, going forth in some manner of worship. Even the menacing looking man who'd caught Maiya's attention earlier was in active worship.

Maiya danced in God's presence for a long time that night. He answered her prayers in abundance. His Word to her was exactly what her soul needed.

When Maiya's praise eventually settled down, Apostle Martin grabbed her hand and hugged her like a father for a few minutes. He pulled away and looked her in the eye. "Daughter, you must keep moving. I know you're hurting, but you must keep moving. The life that is in you can't exist in a dead place! You must come forward again."

Maiya nodded, receiving every last word he said, soaking them up like a sponge.

Once he finished ministering to her, Apostle Martin directed his words to the congregation again. "People of God, you don't have to stay in the place that you're in. God wants you to live and live more abundantly! He wants you to be free! As the song says, it's a new season. It's a new day. A fresh anointing is coming your way. A season of power and prosperity. It's a new season and it's coming your way," he said, quoting the lyrics of a popular Gospel song by Israel and New Breed.

Maiya received those words as well. "Yes!" she shouted and jumped up and down again.

"It is time to get back to the Lord's work and press into Him," Apostle Martin continued. "This time it will not be like before." He pointed from the left to the right side of the sanctuary. "There is something greater waiting for you that you've never experienced before! What you've been through didn't kill you. It wounded you, but it did not, *could* not kill you. God is saying, I'm healing your wounds and your life is still worth living. Tonight is the night that you declare your own prison break!"

"I declare my own prison break!" Maiya shouted along with the rest of the congregation.

And it was so.

CHAPTER TWENTY-THREE
A New Day

Tony recommended a family that would be interested in buying the Cadillac from Maiya. However, she decided not to sell it. Since it was paid in full, she gifted it to the family instead. It was a blessing to be able to do so.

After being told about their recent near-death experience in a major car accident and subsequent losses, Maiya was sure that her decision was the right one. She also assured the family that the maintenance would be complimentary of Tony's company. He was in agreement with that as well since he knew the family personally.

The sale of Maiya's old house was handled just as quickly by Janine and her team. They made the process as seamless as possible for her and the children. They also found them another beautiful home with six bedrooms and seven bathrooms in Conyers, Georgia. It was four thousand square feet of wonderfulness.

Maiya's favorite place in the house was the massive family room that everyone loved to gather in. Although the walls were painted in a very calming sandy earth tone, she added a variety of furniture, pillows, and throw rugs that gave the room a feel of vibrancy.

That same vibrancy was flowing in Maiya's life as well. She was more than happy that God had restored her strength and given her a great support system. She needed both to be able to follow through with the necessary legal process to be completely free from Napoleon. The fact that she was able to recover most of the money that he took added to her happiness.

Maiya still didn't know what happened to cause Dwayne to step up and tell the truth, but she was sure glad he did. His testimony helped to seal the return of that money. Maybe he had a change of heart. She prayed that he did.

Now six weeks after that powerful tag team service, Maiya stood at the counter of the spacious master bathroom in her new home. The stark white walls were covered with splashes of purple, gray, and blue accessories along with a variety of wall décor. That color theme flowed throughout the entire home. The soft lavender bulbs that she chose for the bathroom lighting made it very peaceful and serene to her. These days she went out of her way to promote serenity in every area of her life.

As Maiya prepared for the national conference, she called to check on the kids. They'd spent the night at Jasmine's house. They had grown to adore her over the last few months.

When Maiya was certain that her babies were fine, she made a mental note to call and check on them again once she got settled at the conference center. After all they'd seen her go through lately; she tried to stay in contact with them as much as possible. It was her way of making doubly sure that those troubled times had no lasting effect on them.

"All right, Maiya, it's a new day," she said, giving herself a pep talk as she finished her makeup. "Things have changed. You have changed." Maiya smiled at her reflection in the mirror. "Today is the day, God. Thank You." She looked upward for a few solemn moments.

When Maiya's gaze eventually returned to the mirror, she scanned her attire. The wide-legged, chocolate-colored pants and bell-sleeved purple wrap shirt looked impeccable on her. Though she was still smaller than she used to be before her turmoil, the weight loss actually looked good on her. She was maintaining it in a healthy manner by eating right and exercising. She even managed to get the team to workout with her a few times. Now they were all much slimmer and fit.

Grabbing her purple makeup bag, Maiya turned off the lights as she exited the bathroom. She felt much better about herself and life. She knew it was her time and her turn.

Bouncing happily down the stairs, Maiya ran her hand along the cherry wood banister. She headed to the family room to gather the rest of her things. It was almost time to head to the large auditorium where the conference was being held. She could have stayed at the hotel with the other speakers, but her new home had become her sanctuary. She was more comfortable here and she needed that peace before this assignment.

When Maiya rounded the corner and stepped into the family room, she saw some familiar faces. She burst out laughing. "I'm really going to take my keys back from y'all," she told Van and Angie, who were there waiting for her. "I know I said I would meet y'all there."

"Yeah, yeah, yeah, we know," Angie said, jumping up excitedly from the huge comfortable chair she sat in. "But we wanted to go with you. This is a new day for you!" She smiled as she unknowingly confirmed what Maiya just said to herself only moments before. "So let's go, lady." She grabbed Maiya's arm and pulled her toward the door.

"But what about my stuff?" Maiya protested as she was led away. "I need my Bible and notes."

"I have already put your things in my truck. And, yes, I'm driving you," Van said firmly before she could protest further.

"Well, all right. Let's go then! We've got work to do!" Maiya said excitedly. They wouldn't get any more arguments from her today.

"Everyone else is already there. They are waiting on us," Angie told her.

"Janine too?" Maiya asked, referring to their newest team member.

"Yes!" Angie and Van answered happily in unison.

"And she's excited too. She couldn't stop talking about it at home. So come on, lady, before I get blessed out for making you late." Van chuckled as he turned and walked out the door ahead of them.

Maiya paused for a moment to set the alarm. Then she and Angie followed him out the door.

When they were settled in the truck, Van pulled out of the driveway and headed for the conference. He put on some soothing music. The first song that played was very timely. It was *Moving Forward* by Israel Houghton.

Sitting in the backseat alone, Maiya rested her head against the cool leather and hummed along with the song. She eventually closed her eyes. *Lord, thank You,* she prayed, indulging in peaceful thoughts before she dozed off.

* * * * *

Twenty minutes into their drive, Angie looked in the backseat and saw Maiya dozing. "You know she's about to go ham, right? I can't wait!" she said, laughing quietly.

"Oh yeah, she's going to be going hard in the paint as she likes to say," Van responded through a light chuckle.

"Bishop Horton called earlier to ask how she was doing. He was truly concerned about her," Angie told him.

Van glanced in the rearview mirror before he spoke again.

"Yes, I know. I'm just glad he's such a man of integrity. When you-know-who called him trying to slang mud on Maiya again, he shut him down," Van said in a quiet, whispered tone.

"Ah...I can hear y'all talking about me," Maiya said, slightly opening her eyes. "And you don't have to whisper. I know!" she added, shocking both of them. "Bishop Horton called me too after he talked to you-know-who again. He also made it clear to me that there was no backing out of this conference." She closed her eyes again.

"Well, I guess she told us," Angie said as they laughed together. "Since you can hear us so well, hear this – we're glad he called you. We thought we were going to have to tie you up and drag you there for a while."

"Look at what God has done!" Van responded excitedly. "Well, I guess I should tell you the other news too. You're going to know later on today anyway." He looked at Maiya in the rearview mirror again.

"Tell me what?" Maiya lifted her left brow, yet her eyes remained closed.

"Bishop has commissioned me to share fifteen minutes of empowerment today," Van said.

"HA!" Maiya sprang up in her seat, fully opening her eyes in time to see his wide smile in the mirror. "Let me tell you something, Mr. Empowerment – I already knew that too!" She laughed out loud. "I'm the one that suggested it since you-know-who is no longer on or connected to this team in any way."

Van swerved. His mouth hung open. His eyes instantly filled with tears.

"Excuse me, but neither one of y'all are going to be saying anything if you don't quit swerving. And quit that crying. You're going to make me ruin all this pretty makeup I have on," Angie playfully chided Van as she dabbed at the tears that sprung up in her own eyes. "By the way, Van. I knew too!" She laughed and wiped away more tears.

"So y'all got me this time." Van shook his head. "Well, thank you. I am truly grateful to two of my favorite women in the world."

"I'm not the only one who is called to this. We *all* are," Maiya said seriously.

"I told you," Angie said, "she's about to go ham!"

They all laughed loudly and joyfully.

When they finally made it to their destination, Van pulled up to the speaker's entrance so that Maiya could get to her first meet and greet of the day with the other speakers.

"I'll be in as soon as I park," he said as he ushered them out of the car. "You two need to go ahead. I'll bring everything in with me. Someone will be waiting for you inside."

Angie and Maiya were still laughing as they exited the vehicle.

"Thank you." Maiya looked at Angie with a wide smile and added, "For everything."

"You're welcome," Angie replied, winking her right eye.

They locked arms and walked into the building. They were ready to do what God called them to do. It was their season.

"Good morning, I'm…" Maiya's words quickly trailed off. Although the entryway was literally breathtaking with its warm neutral colors accented by purple and gold carpeting, it was the peace that she felt that caused her to stop so abruptly.

"Prophetess Jackson," said the gorgeous brown-eyed young lady that confidently completed her sentence. "I visit your website often and follow you on social media," she explained. "My name is LaJosie. I'll be your guide for today."

"Well, thank you very much, LaJosie," Maiya said, immediately settling into the peace that seemed to envelope her. "Please forgive my rudeness. This place is so...so beautiful." She continued to admire the elegance of the building. The African artifacts and original paintings that lined the walls were simply exquisite.

"No problem. I understand. This place is *absolutely* beautiful." LaJosie smiled. "Bishop Horton and the others are waiting for you. We can stop by your dressing room, so you'll know where it is. Then I'll take you to them."

"Okay, that would be great. This is Angie," Maiya said, pausing briefly. "One of my ministry partners," she added, letting Angie know in an unconventional way that God had promoted her.

Angie stared at her in shock.

"Hi, Angie." LaJosie extended her right hand in greeting. "Nice to meet you."

"Oh, I'm sorry," Angie said, blinking to refocus. "Hi, LaJosie, nice to meet you, too." She shook the hand offered to her.

"Angie, you are welcome to go upstairs where the ministry teams are if you like," LaJosie said.

"Thank you. I'd like that," Angie answered. "Van, our motivational team lead, is on his way in also with Prophetess Jackson's bags. I'm sure he'd like to go up with me."

"I'll send a text message right now to the other greeter that is also assigned to that entrance." LaJosie pulled her cell phone from her jacket pocket. "I'll make sure she knows to show Van where Prophetess Jackson's things should be taken and to bring him up to the top level where you and the rest of your team will be."

"LaJosie, Van is actually our other ministry partner." Maiya smiled, shocking Angie yet again. "Ha! I got y'all back," she teased her new partner.

"Well, I receive it! Thank you." Angie grinned from ear to ear. "Does Van know?" she inquired excitedly while they waited for LaJosie to finish sending her text message.

"He will when he's introduced tonight." Maiya clapped with a super-sized smile on her face.

"Okay, ladies, I have taken care of it. Van will be properly guided in," LaJosie said. She tucked her phone back into her pocket. "We are good to go now."

"Thank you, LaJosie," Maiya said appreciatively.

"You're most welcome." LaJosie smiled and then led them down the hallway.

"Oh, Maiya, Van loves this ministry so much and he has so many good ideas. Girl, he's not going to be able to talk when he finds out," Angie gushed with teary eyes as they followed LaJosie. "You're gonna mess him up and Janine is gonna shout all over this place. I can't wait!"

Maiya smiled and lifted her right eyebrow. "Van – Mr. Motivation himself? Mess up? Never! He's going to be great!"

"I know that's right," Angie agreed. They slapped each other a high-five.

LaJosie smiled back at them, having heard their cheerful banter. "Here we are, ladies," she said, opening the door to Maiya's designated space. "Prophetess Jackson, if I'm not being too forward, I have to tell you that you all are such an encouragement to me. In the six years I've worked these types of events, I haven't seen many people who are so involved or so kind to their team members. Please don't ever change that."

"Thank you, LaJosie. Who do you work with?" Maiya asked. She liked the young woman's forward, yet cordial demeanor and her kind eyes. She also liked how quickly she handled the matter with Van.

"I work for the conference center as an usher or greeter when needed for different events," LaJosie responded.

"Angie, please get her number," Maiya said as they left her dressing room a few minutes later.

"Are you thinking what I'm thinking?" Angie asked.

"Gatekeeper?" Maiya responded.

"Yes!" Angie said happily. They were with one accord.

"I tell you what, partner. You talk to Ms. LaJosie and if you say she's in, then she's in," Maiya said, inviting Angie further into her new role while LaJosie looked on with open interest and mounting excitement.

"For real?" Angie smiled wide.

"Yes, ma'am. This new hire would be under your supervision also." Maiya winked.

"Thanks, Maiya, we'll have an answer by the end of the week. Tonight we've got work to do," Angie said.

"Alrighty, Ms. LaJosie, if you're interested, please make sure Angie gets your information and she'll be in touch," Maiya said.

"Oh yes, ma'am. I'm *definitely* interested. Thank you so much. Thank You, Jesus!" LaJosie's eyes shined with even more excitement. "Right now I've got to get you to the gathering room. Angie, I'll take you upstairs once we leave Prophetess with the others." She wiped tears from her eyes and led them farther down the hallway.

"LaJosie, we can talk a little more about the position on the way up," Angie said from behind them.

"Yes, ma'am. That would be great," LaJosie responded and then turned to address Maiya. "Prophetess, this is where the meet and greet is being held." She stopped and opened another door for her.

"Thank you, LaJosie. Angie, I'll check in with you later," Maiya said, waving goodbye as she turned to leave them.

Seconds later, Maiya walked into a room that was ballroom size. The crystal chandeliers seemed to shine extra bright to her. The sheer beauty of the room was great, but the love that she was greeted with was greater. Everyone seemed to have genuine smiles and warm words of welcome for the newcomer – her!

Maiya stood in silence for a few moments. This was incredibly humbling and slightly intimidating for her. For some unknown reason, she still had a hard time accepting that people received and honored her labor in the Kingdom. She was still learning to receive in all capacities.

"Prophetess Jackson, welcome to our forum. It is so good to see you again," Bishop Horton said as he approached her. He briefly hugged her like a father would hug a beloved daughter.

"We've all heard so many awesome things about you and your ministry. We are so glad you have agreed to be with us," another person said in greeting. His nametag said Pastor Nielson.

"Thank you so much for having me, but please, call me Maiya," she said.

"Hold on, Prophetess. We believe in giving honor where honor is due. Your work speaks for itself. The manifested words that you've declared into people's lives speak for what God does through you. We understand it's not about the title, but it is who you are," another panel member quickly corrected her. The woman's nametag said Prophetess Means.

Maiya recognized that name as belonging to an anointed, powerhouse of a preacher that she'd heard about. "Yes, ma'am," she said humbly, only slightly shocked by the woman's words and the authority they were spoken with as more recognition set in. Based on what she'd heard of the woman and now experienced for herself, Prophetess Means was definitely a firecracker.

"Thank you for that. You don't quite know what you just did for me with those words," Maiya continued, feeling empowered by that statement.

Bishop Horton didn't address the matter further. He looked satisfied by their exchange. "Is there anything we can get you?" he asked Maiya, looking equally thrilled that she even showed up today. Ordeals like the one she conquered could completely strip a person's self-esteem and confidence away. Some people never made it out.

"Yes, water please," Maiya answered quickly, needing something to quell her nerves as the gravity of where she was today started to sink in.

Amazingly enough, she didn't need that water after all. As Maiya was introduced individually to the other conference speakers, she sensed and enjoyed the camaraderie in the room. She was encouraged by each person there. She listened as they shared their stories and began to understand even more that God meant for her to be here. She needed to meet these people.

Thank You, God, for all that You're doing in me and for putting me in a safe place, Maiya silently prayed. *I am going to have to get with my partners so we can finally get our conference up and rolling. It's been halted long enough,* she thought with even more resolve.

"Please return to the ballroom one hour before the final evening service for intercessory prayer," Bishop Horton said as he concluded their meeting a few minutes later.

Maiya and the others headed back to their individual rooms. The leaders of the breakout sessions had already been released to greet their session attendees. The remaining speakers were encouraged to attend the breakout sessions of their choice throughout the day.

Wow, God. Not bad so far. I need to check in with Angie and see how things are going for them upstairs, Maiya thought, feeling stronger than she had in months.

CHAPTER TWENTY-FOUR
Necessary Forgiveness

Maiya sighed with contentment when she returned to her spacious dressing room. It had a homelike feel to it. She liked the variation of flowers that were placed on the tables and in the corners of the room. She especially loved the mirrored walls and the beautiful, multi-colored plush pillows that were in all the chairs.

Taking a seat in the gorgeous cream-colored lounging chair in the far right corner of the room, Maiya kicked off her 4" brown and gold stilettos, and then retrieved her phone from her purse. She read a few messages from Angie, telling her how things were going upstairs. She responded to the messages and then called the kids.

They picked up where they left off earlier; talking about all the fun they had the night before with Jasmine and how much they loved their newest babysitter. They hung up with heartfelt I-love-yous and promises to see each other and talk more after the service.

Maiya's phone rang immediately after that call ended. It registered an unknown number.

"Hey, baby." It was him – Napoleon.

"Boy, please. That works for those other people. Not over here, not anymore," Maiya responded calmly.

"Ah, girl, you used to love when I called you that," he said smugly. "Besides I'm still your husband."

"Ah, *boy*," Maiya emphasized. "You are quite mistaken. That marriage has been officially over for a while now," she informed in a serious tone.

"Yeah right, Maiya." Napoleon huffed. "Last I heard, you filed for divorce right after I left, but you never followed through with it. Which means you're *still* mine and you still *want* to be mine."

Maiya scoffed. "You're mistaken yet again. I finally closed that chapter six weeks ago. The courthouse has the records whenever you'd like to pick up your copy. Now what do you really want, Napoleon? You have sixty seconds before the phone hangs up on you."

"Whatever, Maiya. I just called because today is the big day, ain't it?" His voice was laced with sarcasm and barely disguised jealousy.

"Actually, yes it is...for both of us. It's the first day of the rest of the best days of my life. It's also the last day you'll ever talk to me," she said firmly.

"Oh, so you're brand new now. It's not going to last long, Maiya. You have got to know that I've told all of them about you. When I get done, it's going to be worse than you ever thought, because I'm not going to stop. You'll never be bigger than I am in ministry. I am the Bishop!" Napoleon yelled, continuing his hateful tirade. "I am—"

"Ah, Napoleon," Maiya said, calmly interrupting him.

"You need to address me as *Bishop* Napoleon!" he shouted.

"Ha!" Maiya laughed out loud. "Okay, *Bishop*, Napoleon and whatever else you'd like to be called, I forgive you."

"Yeah whatever, Maiya. You ain't all that! Who do you think you are anyway? *You* forgive *me*? Whatever," he said, feigning laughter.

Maiya let her silence answer him.

"Humph. What? No cussing today? You mean that's all that you have to say to me?" Napoleon instigated.

"Yes. Really, I forgive you. I forgive you and this is over." Maiya smiled, pleased that she still felt so calm. She didn't feel any anger or rage, only laughter. She knew he was incensed because he couldn't get a rise out of her.

"It was over when I let your wannabe ass go," Napoleon responded angrily, proving what she already knew to be true. He was trying to goad her into a fight on such a pivotal day for her and so many others.

"No," Maiya said quickly. She paused to choose her next words wisely. "It was over when *I* let *you* go. I had to release you from my mind, my heart, and my soul. For the last time, I forgive you, Napoleon. I pray that God has mercy on you. Goodbye." Then she pressed the end call button on her phone. When it immediately rang again, she sent the call directly to voicemail, and then placed the phone face down on the gray marble countertop near her seat.

"Thank You, Jesus." Maiya lifted her right hand in praise. She jumped up and darted around the room in a sprint. "Glory!" she shouted, smoothly going into her praise dance. She couldn't hold it in and she didn't want to. She was happy in Jesus.

Ten minutes later, Maiya finally sat back down, still smiling and rejoicing inside. She laid her head on the chair's comfortable headrest, closed her eyes and focused her thoughts on the impartation that she was charged to deliver that night. Her assignment was to minister to God's people about restoration. God had restored her and she was excited to share what she learned first-hand about what He was able to do.

During that time of meditation, Maiya decided not to attend any of the breakout sessions. Rather she would eat a light lunch with the group. With that decision made, she continued to enjoy the peace and quiet of the room. She also used that time to pray and give God more praise.

"Lord, thank You for allowing me to walk in true forgiveness and for removing all bitterness from me. I ask You to forgive Napoleon because he obviously doesn't know what he's doing. You said in Your Word that the least that is done unto them is done unto You. Have mercy upon him, Lord. I pray that something is said to him that will help him turn back to You. Lord, thank You so much that You love me and didn't let me stay in the place I was in. Thank You, God, for not erasing my future because of my past. In Jesus Name. Amen! Hallelujah!"

After more time of prayer and meditation, Maiya read over her notes. The message had truly ministered to her as she was preparing it in the preceding weeks. She jotted down additional things that the Lord was ministering to her right then, in case she needed them later.

Once she finished reviewing her notes, Maiya placed the notebook, along with her Bible, on the counter beside her phone. She slipped her feet back into her shoes and got up. She was ready to fellowship some more.

Before Maiya turned to leave, she noticed the black and gold sign that hung above the counter. It read – *Forgiveness Yields Freedom. Free Yourself.*

The beautiful calligraphy is what initially grabbed her attention. Yet it was the truth of the words that deeply penetrated her soul. She smiled wide and felt even more peace concerning her vital decision to forgive those who'd hurt her.

After double-checking her appearance in the floor length mirror to her left, Maiya headed for the door. Just as she grabbed the doorknob, she heard her phone ring again. She recognized Israel Houghton's *Moving Forward* ringtone as that of her ministry line.

Maiya started not to answer it. It might be Napoleon and she didn't have any more time to give to his mess. However, she doubled back just to make sure she didn't miss a true ministry call. When she picked up the phone from the counter and saw the Caller ID, she smiled.

"Well hello, Minister Charlene," Maiya enthusiastically greeted her. They hadn't talked in quite a while.

"Hi, Prophetess. I hope I didn't reach you at a bad time. I've got so much to tell you," Charlene responded excitedly.

"Now is a great time. I'm all ears." Maiya kicked off her stilettos again and returned to the comfy chair. Lunch could wait. This was more important to her.

"Oh my! Where do I start? Okay, first let me tell you that things have drastically changed in my household," Charlene said, speaking in her usual hurried manner. "My husband has completely turned around. Now he's supportive, loving, kind, and he's active in church. We're even working with some ministries together."

"That is wonderful. Praise the Lord! God is able!" Maiya said, sharing in her joy.

"Yes, ma'am. The Lord did it because I was done! I put him out and everything. Well, at least I tried to. When he got out of jail and the hospital, I let him back in. But that's a totally different story and too long to share right now. Anyway we went to this service a short while ago and it was amazing. These two brothers were preaching and God used them mightily. Prophetess, God changed and delivered my husband that very night. Before then, he was full of rage and anger, and he was taking it out on everyone – especially me."

Maiya listened quietly to Charlene's happy recital of events. Her mind started putting two and two together.

"Oh my God," Charlene continued, almost without taking a breath. "I can't even explain to you how awesome that night was. How it drastically changed our lives. I was terrified when I got to the church. I thought my husband was going to kill me. Earlier that day, I literally begged him to let me go, but he protested. He thought I was messing around with the preachers. I'm new to the Atlanta area and so I didn't even know them. I kept telling him that my cousin invited me. When she kept raving about how good the service was going to be, I felt like I needed to be there, so I left the house and went. Long story short, he followed me there. Thank Jesus that he did, because he is now a changed man." Her voice cracked as the words rapidly gushed out. She sounded like she was crying...crying happy tears this time.

Maiya's smile widened as even more pieces to the puzzle fell into place. Now she understood why she couldn't keep her eyes off of that lady in blue and the menacing looking man at that tag team service. *God, You are absolutely amazing*, she thought.

"Charlene, the night that you are referring to. Was it a tag team service?" Maiya asked, though she already knew the answer to her question.

"Yes, how did you know?" Charlene asked hesitantly.

"I was there also. I saw you, but at the time I didn't know it was you. You were wearing all blue. I saw your husband sitting next to you. He was mean-mugging in a big way," Maiya explained.

"Wow! So did you see the lady that the Pastor was prophesying to? He was running across chairs trying to get to her," Charlene said excitedly. "I've never seen anything like that in my life. It was so intense. There were so many people crowded around, so I couldn't see who he was talking to, but I did see her take off running in a blur. That lady was moving so fast. It started a wild fire in there. People were everywhere. Literally, all you could see were people shouting, arms flinging, hair slinging and more people running." Her voice elevated a full octave in her excitement.

"Ha!" Maiya laughed. "Charlene, that lady was me," she confessed.

"Shut the front door! That was *you* running like a track star? Wow! Well all right then. We were in the same place and didn't even know it," Charlene said with wonder in her voice.

"Yes," Maiya replied, "but it sounds like the both of us received exactly what we needed that night. I'm really happy to hear that your marriage is working out well. I praise God for the restoration He has given you and your husband! Our God is able to do anything but fail!" As she spoke, she couldn't contain her grin.

"We are still in counseling, but I am so happy now," Charlene said, sounding as happy as she claimed. "We started out going to three sessions a week. Now we're going two days a week along with a group therapy session and it's definitely helping. God has truly transformed us both. We are even sharing our testimony for the first time next weekend at a Domestic Violence event. Pray for us. It's going to be hard having to be so transparent, but I'm ready."

Maiya loved hearing the joy that radiated through her quickly spoken words. "I will definitely do that. By the way, if my memory serves me correctly, I thought you lived in Indiana. Have you moved to Georgia? Or were you just visiting that night?"

"We actually live in the Atlanta area now. We've been here for the last three months. In fact, I have a hot date tonight with my hubby at a quaint bistro in Midtown." Charlene giggled like a schoolgirl.

Maiya chuckled. "That's great! Enjoy yourself. And thank you so much for calling and sharing your testimony with me. It encouraged me tremendously. God bless and please keep in touch," she said as they ended the call on a joyous note.

"Well, Lord, You've done it again! You are so mighty, God! Thank You for Your restoring power, Lord. Thank You, Jesus!" Maiya clapped, taking a moment to praise God yet again.

When she settled down once more, she wiped the tears that had formed in the corners of her eyes. After putting her shoes back on, she got up even more joyful than before, and then went to meet the group for lunch.

CHAPTER TWENTY-FIVE
Freedom

Seated on the stage, Maiya listened to Van share his motivational moment. She grinned like a Cheshire cat, remembering the look on his face when Bishop Horton introduced him as a ministry partner. It was priceless. She thought he was going to take off running. Instead he did a two-step dance when he took the microphone. They were all going to have some laughs together about that later.

Seems like somebody else is going ham tonight, Maiya thought happily concerning Van's message. *I knew he could do it, Lord.*

"Remember that if you take the limits off of God, the limits will be taken off of you. You can, because God can! I'm Van Taylor and it's been my honor to share this motivational moment with you tonight. God bless you!" Van concluded, lifting his hands in praise as he turned to walk to the back of the stage. He smiled toward Maiya as he walked off.

She gave him a thumbs-up sign and a huge grin. She stood and applauded him along with everyone else.

Soon the worship team began ministering William Murphy's – *It's Working*. That song was so befitting following Van's timely word of motivation. His words reminded Maiya that all things work together for our good when we love God and are called according to His purpose. She remained standing and worshipped as the worship team continued to set the atmosphere for the rest of the service.

At times Maiya watched the crowd. Other times she closed her eyes in meditation. She thanked God for enlarging her territory as she stood ready to pour into people of all nationalities, cities, age groups, social and economic backgrounds. God's Word concerning her was manifesting right before her eyes. His promise, which had become her dream, was finally coming to pass. It was working for her good.

Bishop Horton returned to the podium immediately following the worship team. It was time for his opening statements of the night and more introductions.

As he spoke, Maiya pondered the Word she was about to share. Her thoughts were interrupted when he began to introduce her. Bishop Horton spoke as though they'd known each other for a lifetime. She smiled gratefully, encouraged by his words.

"Ladies and gentlemen, I feel like a proud father tonight as I introduce this great woman of God," Bishop Horton said. "I have witnessed her transformation. I have followed her ministry for quite a long time and I must say that she is the real deal. She's raw. She's truthful and very transparent. She's full of the Holy Ghost and she is approved by God."

Maiya smiled wider. It seemed that Van and Angie weren't the only ones with a great surprise tonight. She had no idea that Bishop Horton esteemed her so highly.

Lord Jesus, thank You so much, Maiya prayed, dropping her head briefly in gratitude. She was especially grateful for the added comfort Bishop Horton's words brought to her as she prepared to minister.

Maiya needed that comfort now more than ever before. Not just because she occasionally still dealt with feelings of unworthiness due to her past, but also because she'd been put through some awful things and hadn't been completely blameless herself. Knowing that God was still willing to use her was humbling. She had been through the process. It was her time to walk in the promise.

Maiya lifted her head and continued listening to the man of God's amazing introduction.

"I could tell you many more things about her, but what's most important is that her love for God and His people are real," Bishop Horton continued. "Her heart towards the healing of God's people is authentic. If you came to hear from God tonight, I believe this awesome Word carrier is going to impart into us exactly what God has poured into her. I really could talk about her for a long time, but I won't. You're about to see for yourselves." He turned to Maiya with a huge smile. "Prophetess Jackson, what we need today is in you. We are ready to hear the voice of God through you."

Maiya smiled as she got up from her seat and walked towards Bishop Horton. She paused to return the fatherly hug he gave her on the way to the front of the stage.

"You made it through. It's time to pull someone else out tonight," Bishop Horton whispered to her.

When Maiya approached the podium, she saw that her Bible and notebook had already been placed there earlier by Angie. She looked across the large auditorium again.

Maiya's smile widened when she spotted Mama Ludie and Star seated on the front row of the left section on the lower level. They were smiling and worshipping along with everyone else. They waved to one another in acknowledgement.

Maiya continued to span the massive room looking at the many people that God had gathered together. For some unknown reason, her eyes settled on the last seat on the front row of the center aisle. When she saw who was there, the reason was clear and she understood better.

Taking the cordless microphone from the stand, Maiya began to sing her newest song – *Free*. She penned it a few weeks before the conference. The talented musicians quickly picked up the tune on their instruments and flowed with her. It was absolutely dynamic. Quietness instantly spread across the massive auditorium as she sang.

"No longer bound," Maiya sang slowly, walking toward the stairs to the left of the stage. Her first alto voice was melodic and rich in tone. "No longer chained. No longer down. I'm free. Free to be me. Whom the Son sets free is free indeed. Oh, I'm free. I'm free to be me."

Maiya walked in the opposite direction of the place where her eyes had settled only moments prior. There was no reason to alarm the person she'd spotted.

"Musicians, please keep playing. People of God, let's worship the Lord our God. He is great and greatly to be praised," Maiya exhorted, stopping right in front of an unsuspecting Allysa – another person she needed to forgive completely. She turned her microphone off and handed it to the usher that stood next to Allysa.

Allysa's head was bowed down. Her shoulders were slumped over. Tears flowed down her face staining her crimson and white blouse.

Maiya grabbed her shaking hands and gently pulled her up from her seat.

Allysa lifted her head slightly, revealing red swollen eyes.

"Daughter, I love you and I forgive you," Maiya said, continuing to hold her hands and speak life into her. "You were a victim of someone else's unrepentant evil and unfortunately, you weren't strong enough to resist. The enemy set you up to destroy you. Today the Lord says you're being set free. From this day forward, forgive yourself. It's time to come out of this self-imposed prison that you've been in."

Allysa's body trembled even more. Her tears refused to abate.

"Hold your head up, princess, and know that all is well," Maiya continued to encourage her. "There is still greatness in you and there is a place for you in God's Kingdom to do the work assigned to you. He will put you where He wants you to be. You must remember that your gifts will make room for you and bring you before great men. Make sure you use those gifts for Him."

"Thank you," Allysa whispered, "I will."

Maiya smiled at her. Then she kissed both of her cheeks before turning to walk away. After thanking the usher for holding the microphone, she headed back to the stage. She turned the microphone back on and started to sing again.

Maiya's team and Bishop Horton watched from their respective places in the room with teary eyes. They knew the intricate details of that matter as well as the necessity of what she had just done.

"Come on and bless the wonderful Name of Jesus in this place," Maiya said, walking up the stairs, smiling at the greatness of the Lord.

As she returned to the stage, she saw people in the crowd weeping. She could see spiritual chains and shackles falling off of many. Others still appeared to be weighted down...but prayerfully not for long.

"I know you all didn't hear what I said to our young sister just now, but I want to encourage you. Even though the enemy set you up and tried to enslave you and destroy your life, this is the day that God wants you to be free. I know what it's like to be trapped. I've been entangled. Shame and embarrassment had me imprisoned. But now I make the daily declaration over my own life that I am free in Jesus Name. I'm free to be me," Maiya said, returning to the podium.

She began to sing more of *Free*.

"I'm made in His image, shaped by His hand, covered by His blood, redeemed by His love. I'm free. I'm free to be me." Maiya ended the song after singing the second stanza. She was ready to begin a different kind of impartation. The forgiveness she extended toward Allysa was for her as well. It unleashed even more freedom within her.

She smiled wide as she offered the Lord her own worship. "The Spirit of the Lord is here. The great I AM. The Lover of our souls. The Redeemer of our lives – He is here," Maiya continued. "God is moving in this place! His Word is about to change our lives forever. Come on and put your hands together if you are believing God for your change."

Maiya waved her left hand high above her head. She was absolutely in love with Jesus. It took all the restraint she had to contain the holler that was already rising up in her spirit. She had to remain focused to deliver this message.

All over the building people were offering up praise. Hallelujah, Thank You, Lord and Praise Jesus were frequently uttered, among other praises. The few minutes that passed were glorious.

"Hallelujah!" Maiya shouted. "I feel a press in my spirit. This is not playtime. This is real! Yes, Lord! There is a Word from God and He wants to set us at liberty. The Bible teaches us that where the Spirit of the Lord is, there is liberty. Liberty is in the building tonight. Oh glory! Don't miss it.

Don't miss God tonight!"

Maiya walked around to the front of the podium and stood at the edge of the stage. It was about to be a different kind of night. She'd heard the Lord say in her spirit – *Connect with them.*

"I can see in the spirit the chains and shackles that have some of you bound, but the presence of the Lord is here," Maiya shared. "The Lord sees the spiritual sickness of many of you. Some of you seem to be at the point of death, but tonight there is life for you." She paused, listening intently for more leading from the Holy Spirit.

"The brokenhearted have come looking for a way in and a way out," she continued. "Some of you are stuck in the wrong relationship. Meanwhile, your relationship with Christ has dwindled to almost nothing. Freedom is in this house tonight! The Deliverer wants to pull you out of bondage and usher you into life. Is anybody ready to receive it tonight?" Maiya held the microphone away from her, pointing towards the crowd.

The crowd and those on the podium responded with, "Amen. Hallelujah!"

Many people stood with their hands lifted in praise. Others worshipped silently with streams of tears running down their faces.

Maiya watched all this, determined to stay completely in tune with the Spirit of God. It was too crucial. Lives were at stake. These were more than just people filling a room.

Maiya sensed deliverance hovering in the atmosphere. Although there was a war going on within some people, the peace of God was like a shadow waiting to envelope them.

Behind her on the stage, she heard words of encouragement. She was happy to have the support and love that was being shown. However, her only goal at that pivotal moment was for them to experience God and hear His voice.

"I hear the Spirit of the Lord saying...Pray," Maiya shared. "Kind Father, in the Name of Jesus, we thank You. God, I come before You tonight asking for Your presence to saturate us. We pray for Your anointing that destroys the yokes, breaks up fallow ground and sets captives free. Father, we are in need of Your restoration in our lives. Spirit of the Living God, speak to these Your children. Allow this Word to change our lives forever. God, we glorify You, we magnify You, we exalt You and we love You. We believe that Your Word is true and that You will perform it. In Jesus Name we pray. And all that love God, shout Hallelujah!" she said, ending the prayer on a high note.

"Hallelujah!" rang out all over the building.

Maiya walked back to the podium and flipped open her Bible and notebook. "Let us look into the Word for what else God wants to say to us tonight," she began. "I want to draw your attention to Jeremiah, the twenty-ninth chapter, verses ten through fourteen. I'll give you a few moments to find it. Say amen, if you have it. Or wait on me, if you don't. I'd rather wait on you now rather than let you get left later."

"Amen," rang out from the majority of the crowd.

Some said, "Wait on me."

Maiya paused briefly to allow those who needed more time to locate the scripture reference for the message.

"The Word from the Lord tonight is Restoration is Coming!" Maiya looked upward and added in silent prayer, *Have Your way, Lord.*

CHAPTER TWENTY-SIX
Restoration Is Coming

"To God be the glory. Restoration is coming!" Maiya said. Then after reading aloud those passages from Jeremiah, she began her message in earnest. "I'm not going to waste any time tonight. There is a prophetic declaration for this hour and the Lord has instructed me to get to it expediently. All I ask is that you pray with me and open your hearts to receive what the Lord has to say."

"Amen," resounded on the stage and in the audience.

"When you think of restoration, you often think of something being given back, being made to look like new or being restored to its original state. If it's a house, you may call it remodeling or renovation. If it's an addict, you may call it rehabilitation or recovery. If it's something torn down, you refer to it as rebuilding and so on and so on. The whole point of restoration is to put something back where it belongs or give something back to its rightful owner. It's a return." Maiya paused and looked out at the crowd.

"God sent me here to tell you that He's about to put you back in your rightful place in the Kingdom," she continued after looking at her notes. "You've been pushed aside, pushed around and pushed to the back long enough. It's time for you to be in your place. The dead season is just about up for you. Beloved, it's almost over."

On the stage behind her, someone shouted, "Glory!"

"The Lord declares that as soon as this season is up, He's going to do just what He said," Maiya continued. "There will be no delay in the manifestation of His promise. You might not understand it all right now. It may appear to be out of order and things may seem to be falling apart, but be assured that God has it all in control. As His Word says in our scripture tonight, He has it all planned out."

"Preach, daughter!" Bishop Horton yelled encouragingly.

"Beloved, God has plans to take care of you," Maiya went on to say. "When you think of taking care of someone or something, you may think of giving them a home, food, clothes, shoes, etcetera. God said, He has already made every provision for you, both now and forever more."

People started to spring up from their seats. Multiple declarations of "Amen," rang out loudly across the building.

"God said, right now, don't miss that. He said, right now He's about to give you back some things that were taken from you and some things that you willingly let go of," Maiya shared.

"Yes!" Van shouted to the left of her on the stage.

"One of the first things God wants to restore to you is your identity. The Lord said, He wants to remind you of who you are. You are fearfully and wonderfully made. You are a royal priesthood and a holy nation. You are an heir of God and a co-heir with Christ Jesus."

"That's the word, preacher!" a lady in the front row yelled, standing on the floor at the edge of the stage.

"The Lord said, let Him restore your confidence. You are the head and not the tail. You are above and not beneath. God said, as a matter of fact, you are like Abigail, you're wise and you're beautiful. You're called like Esther, for such a time as this. You are akin to Deborah, an ordained leader and moreover, you are like Hannah, you have been vindicated by the Lord," Maiya said, the words pouring from her spirit like a faucet on full blast. "Oh come on in here, somebody! Bless His name!"

Clapping and loud shouts of praise were heard throughout the building.

Maiya did her best to stay calm, but it was becoming increasingly difficult to do so. This word penetrated her more now than it had when God first spoke it to her.

Allysa stood to her feet for the first time since Maiya had spoken to her earlier. Her head was bowed, but Maiya discerned that she was nevertheless receiving the word in her own special way.

"Awww, you preaching in here, girl," said a man whose voice boomed above the others.

Maiya recognized that tired drawl from anywhere. It was Napoleon. She didn't flinch. Nor did she give him or his presence a second thought. She kept moving forward, not even slightly affected by him.

"Listen in here, the Lord said, He's getting ready to give you back everything the cankerworm thought he took from you," Maiya declared. "And don't you dare talk yourself out of it. Get your mind off of what you've been through and what you see right now. The Lord said to assure you that because *He* said it, restoration is coming!"

More people popped up across the room. Others, who were still struggling internally, remained seated.

Maiya knew she had to press on because there was a breakthrough waiting to happen for the people on this night.

"The Lord said, He knows that you feel like you've been in the desert or the dry place but because of your faithfulness, He has not forgotten about you. He has seen you when you've prayed and praised your way through. He knows the times when you've been weak and wanted to give up, but He said that He also saw your faith when you kept holding on. He saw you praising your way through. Sons and daughters, because you kept seeking Him out even when you felt like you couldn't find Him, God said to remind you that He is not slack concerning His promises. Beloved, your restoration is coming!"

Thunderous shouts of praise were heard all over the building. Maiya saw one lady take off running across the room.

"There is a scripture in Isaiah 35:2 that says – like a crocus it will burst into bloom. When something bursts, it has either been building under pressure or it appears to happen immediately. God said, He's been building you under the pressure and there are some things, that after this season, He's going to immediately restore to you. Ah yeah, God. I receive that for myself!" Maiya said excitedly.

She paused briefly, picking up more things in her spirit. She needed her thought process to be clear before she went on.

"God said, He's about to call back to life some things that appear to have died in your life," Maiya continued after a moment. "He's about to rejuvenate some of your dreams and passions. Are there any people in the building who will admit that you need restoration?"

She stopped when she heard loud shouts fill the air again. She faintly heard some people shouting, "Restore me."

Others said, "Yes, Lord."

Based on that general consensus, Maiya discerned that the people wanted what God was offering them right now.

"Now wait, there is a word of caution," she said, walking to the front of the stage. "It is not for you to go trying to revive or restore things or people to yourself. God said that this is *His* plan. Some things, some people, some relationships, some businesses and some of your habits – they need to stay buried. But be encouraged because God knows exactly what you need."

Maiya paced back and forth across the stage. "Listen, some of that stuff had to die. It had to so that those things that are sleeping could be awakened in you and live again. God said, you're about to have a Lazarus experience. Whew, Jesus!" She shouted with excitement as that revelation settled in her spirit.

"The same way Jesus specifically called Lazarus out of the grave, there are some specific things He's about to resurrect in your life. There are some specific people that He's about to restore back to your life and there are some specific parts of you that He is calling back to life."

Maiya literally jumped up and down at this point. She paused to catch her breath. She knew she had to finish delivering the message. She knew that every word that God was speaking through her was necessary.

"Come on, people of God, it's time for you to come back!" Maiya jumped up and down again, pointing her right index finger toward the crowd.

All across the building, including the stage, every person stood to their feet. Some of them jumped up and down as well. There wasn't a dry eye in the building.

"Too often, we only see restoration as getting stuff back or having people come back, but God said in this time of restoration, He is calling *you* back!" Maiya continued. "He's calling you to live, to prosper and to be in good health. This restoration is not about what you get or who comes with you. This is about where you've been, what has happened *in* you and where God is getting ready to take you. He said, He had to let you experience this dead season. He had to let all of these things happen. In other words, Uzziah had to die, so you would see Him and Lazarus had to die, so they would believe Him."

More revelation sank into her own soul as she spoke those words. "Oh, dear Jesus. I hear You, God!" Maiya cried out, teetering on the edge of the stage.

Altar workers gathered around the stage on the floor to ensure her safety.

"Oh, my Lord! Jesus!" Maiya shouted as her legs move faster and faster, almost like she was running in place. "Jesus asked Martha – didn't I tell you that if you believe, you would see the glory of God? God was just trying to get you to see the glory! There was a need for you to endure. You had to be tried. These tests were mandatory. The valley, the desert, they were all allowed so you would believe." She paced briskly back and forth again.

Just as quickly, Maiya turned and headed toward the stairs on the right side of the stage.

Angie darted from across the stage and followed her.

Van immediately followed as well.

"Listen to me, beloved. God is saying, now is the time that He wants to restore you." Maiya stopped when she made it to the floor.

Angie and Van stood behind her on the stairs, watching and waiting for her next move.

More shouts of praise were heard all over the building. Some people waved their hands. A few more ran around the open area of the floor.

All of a sudden, Maiya took off walking extremely fast. She moved so fast, it was as if she had on roller skates.

"I hear You, God!" Maiya jumped on top of an empty chair at the end of a row. "Let's get something straight in here. The Lord said, stop letting the enemy rent space in your head that he can't even pay for. How dare you let the devil, who does not even have keys to his own house, have space in yours? Not in here. Not today! The enemy comes but to kill, steal and destroy, but Jesus said, But I Come!"

She paused briefly to let those potent words sink in.

"Listen, listen, listen, the Lord said, get your mind right in here," Maiya continued prophetically. "Jesus said, I came to give you the joy of your salvation back. I came to restore the freedom and ability to love without fear. And I came to give you peace of mind. He said, I come that you might have life and life abundantly!"

Maiya was in rare form as she jumped up and down in the chair. Like Van described earlier that day, she was going hard in the paint.

Many of the attendees gathered around her chair while Van and Angie stood nearby, watching closely. They both wore big cheesy grins on their faces.

"Oh come on now. Don't miss what God is doing in this place. The Spirit of the Lord is saying that He has come to erase the stains that have been left on your heart. He is here to restore the *you* that you lost, the you that died in the midst of all that was going on. Hear the voice of the Lord in here, Lazarus – it's time for you to come forth!"

Maiya looked at those gathered around her as she spoke. "The Lord said, He came to restore you! You, woman of God! You, man of God! You, His vessel, His anointed one! You, His chosen people. It's time for the grave clothes that have been holding you, to loose you and let you go. God said, He's restoring you to your freedom. People of God, declare it with me, restoration is coming!"

"Restoration is coming!" was their echoed reply. The corporate response sounded like a forceful boom throughout the building.

Maiya stilled for a few seconds as the crowd shouted out more praises. She listened intently to the Spirit of God before pressing on further into the message. She shook herself again when she felt a quick check in her spirit.

"Hold up, the Lord said, didn't He just tell you to get your minds right in here?" Maiya stated, posing the question she just heard. "I can hear you in the spirit saying that people have always told you that you would be nothing. That's all that's resonating in your mind. But the devil is a lie. God said, it's time to turn that thing around."

She paused only briefly to take a breath and then went at it again. "Child of God, you must stand up in your authority as a blood bought believer. You have the power in you to turn every ill spoken word against you around for your good. They said, you will never be nothing and they are absolutely right! You will NEVER be nothing! Oh come on here, somebody!" Maiya jumped out of the chair into the midst of the crowd, landing squarely on her feet. She moved so fast that no one had a chance to help her down.

On the move again, she pressed her way through the masses. She walked even faster than before. She was barefoot now. Her stilettos had been left in the chair she once stood in.

Angie immediately retrieved her shoes and handed them off to a trustworthy person.

Van followed Maiya. The crowd dispersed as she walked through.

"With God, I was created for something. I was born to be somebody," Maiya continued. "I was born *on* purpose. I was born *with* a purpose but, baby, I'll never be nothing! In God, I'm free. In God, I'm prosperous. In God, I'm in good health. Come on, decree it over yourself. Say, I'm blessed when I come in and when I go out. I'm the head and not the tail. I'm the lender and not the borrower. I'll always be on top and never on the bottom. I may have been a lot of things, but the one thing I will NEVER be – is NOTHING! Get that deep down in your spirit. Say it over and over again, I'll NEVER be NOTHING!"

"Whew! I'm about to shout myself right there!" Maiya said with an excited chuckle.

Now almost at the back of the auditorium, she saw that the crowd was still standing room only. Most of them turned around. They looked to see which direction she was headed next.

Angie and Van walked to the left and right corners of the room respectively. They continued to watch with careful eyes.

"I don't hear you in here," Maiya continued fervently when very few people uttered those confessions. "You've got to confess this with your *own* mouth tonight! I'm fearfully and wonderfully made. I'm a royal priesthood. I'm a holy nation. I belong to the King. I belong to the Lord. I'm anointed of the Lord. I'm chosen by God. I am His daughter. I am His son. I am loved of the Lord. I'm healed and I'm whole!"

Maiya stopped close to the back of the room, turning around to face the crowd of people still standing. "Come on now. Shouting is good, but you've got to *speak* these things, so you can *see* these things in your own life. The Bible says that if you decree a thing, God will establish it in the earth for you! Decree it for yourself! I will NEVER be NOTHING! Hey glory!"

As the people finally grabbed hold of the need to make these personal confessions over their own lives, Maiya went into a moment of personal praise. Her praise increased with fervor at each resounding confession.

Releasing a loud yell from her belly, Maiya suddenly took off running. She'd just caught sight of someone with her spiritual eyes and felt a sense of urgency concerning that individual. She knew that she had to get to that person...NOW!

CHAPTER TWENTY-SEVEN
Mended Fences

Maiya's spiritual radar kicked into overdrive. She ran up and down each aisle, looking urgently from left to right. She stopped near the tenth row from the very back of the room as another vision flash before her eyes. This one featured more details of the woman she'd seen only seconds prior. The main detail was a purple flower in the woman's hair.

Maiya instinctively reached up and touched her own purple flower. It was her signature piece and she loved wearing it.

She's in here, Maiya heard the Lord say as He gave her even more details about the woman. "Vision Team, I need your help," she called out. Fortunately, they were all on the floor by that time, ready in case she needed help with anything or anyone.

The audience intently watched what was going on via the huge monitors that were positioned high on the left and right walls of the auditorium. The room grew even quieter.

"Musicians, please play something soft for us," Maiya requested. They immediately honored her request.

"There is a woman in this building with a purple flower in her hair. She's brown-skinned with tan-colored pants and a gold-looking shirt on. I need her. Walk the floor. When you see her, bring her to me," Maiya instructed her team as she walked swiftly back up the aisle toward the front.

"Everybody in this room, start praying. We have to find this lady now. She's sitting in here and she hears God, but the spirit of suicide is on her heavily. Come on in here, we've got to take responsibility for one another," Maiya said, enlisting the help of the audience as well.

As the people searched, she paced the floor in front of the stage, praying in the Spirit. The urgency that she felt showed up in her tense body language. Her shoulders felt tight.

The Vision Team members prayed also as they walked around the room. Some of them made it to the upper levels looking for the mystery woman. People in the audience helped them. Even the ministers on the podium helped with the search. Everyone was on one accord.

"Come on, daughter. I see you in the spirit and I hear your heart. Don't you walk out that door!" Maiya stopped in her tracks. "Somebody check the doors. Gatekeepers, if anyone is going out, please look for her among them. This is a matter of life and death," she said, walking toward the back again.

Midway down the aisle, Maiya felt the unction to stop again. She looked around and then turned towards the side exit on the right side of the room. That's when she spotted the lady from behind.

The woman hurried toward the exit with her head bowed and her shoulders slumped over. She was trying to maneuver through the crowd of people gathered near the doors, desperately trying not to be seen.

But she was seen. As if she had eagle's eyes, Maiya saw the woman's profile all the way from where she stood. She couldn't clearly make out her face because her head was bowed extremely low. She saw her shaking profusely. Maiya also discerned that she was trying to run away.

There was something instantly familiar about this woman. *Is it the flower?* Maiya thought. It was identical to hers. *No, God, it's something else.*

Maiya didn't hesitate another second. She didn't want to take a chance on losing her. She took off in an all-out sprint across the auditorium floor.

Gripping the microphone like a relay baton, she pumped her arms up and down as she ran. She closed the distance between them in less than thirty seconds.

Maiya made it to the woman right before she stepped outside the door. Her exit had been deterred by the unending stream of people flooding into the room.

Grabbing the woman's shirt, Maiya pulled her back inside. As their gazes met, revelation slammed into her immediately.

"Nicole?" Maiya gasped sharply. "Dear Lord Jesus." She stared at her biological mother in shock for a few moments. Then she gently embraced her.

Nicole dropped her head immediately. Her shoulders slumped and her tears fell to the floor. "Please let me go, please," she said, barely audible. "I'm sorry. I didn't want you to see me. I didn't come to cause trouble."

"My God," Maiya said, catching her breath. "I heard you in the spirit. You said, 'that sounds good, but you don't know what I've done. The Lord said, He hears you and He knows your pain. He knows what really happened all those years ago. He knows about the betrayal. Beloved, God brought you here tonight to save your life. You can't leave here with this intent to never live again. Nicole, He didn't erase your future because of your past."

"I made life hell for you," Nicole sobbed. Her head still drooped.

Maiya bowed her head, took a deep breath, and regained her composure. Forgiving Allysa and Napoleon was one thing. Now she felt the pressing in her spirit to extend full forgiveness to the first person that ever hurt her. It was necessary for her healing process to be complete. Thanks to God, she was more than ready to extend that and more to Nicole.

"Mother, all is well," Maiya said gently, lifting her head again. "God sees your heart tonight and all is forgiven. He wants you to know that He forgives you and I want you to know that *I* forgive you too. The past is the past and it's time to let it go and move on. Forgive yourself and move on."

Maiya sighed deeply. She'd felt a divine release in her spirit as she spoke those heartfelt words. She wrapped her arms tightly around Nicole and held her for a few more moments. Love and compassion filled her heart for the weary woman.

"Lift up your head. Today is the last day you'll walk around like this. Look at me," Maiya said tenderly as a steady stream of tears flowed down both of their faces. "God loves you dearly."

Nicole fidgeted with her hands and dropped her head again.

Maiya lifted her chin with her hand and embraced her again.

Nicole held on to her tighter than before, perhaps making up for all the years they hadn't hugged at all. Perhaps she just needed someone to hold on to right now.

The tighter Nicole held on to her, the more Maiya sensed the weight of her emotional pain. It was so heavy that they begin to slide to the floor.

As they went down, Bishop Horton, Pastor Nielson, and one of the other podium members rushed to catch them. Van sprinted over to them as well.

Maiya and Nicole crumpled to the floor a split second before any of them could make it in time. It was all right. God had them.

Lifting up her right hand to signal that they were okay, Maiya continued to hold Nicole and rock her in her arms. She handed the microphone that she'd been gripping to Van as he backed away.

"Nicole, God is working tonight! On YOU! While you sat here, while you stood, while you cried, God has been working on your behalf!" Maiya said.

Nicole tightened her grip around Maiya's waist and released a loud high pitched scream.

Maiya continued to hold her. She let her scream as long as she needed to, as loud as she needed to. As God flooded her with revelation concerning her mother, she knew that Nicole needed this release desperately.

Around them people continued to pray. Bishop Horton and Van were the loudest, praying like warriors in their circle of four.

The musicians continued to play softly.

The worship team returned to the stage and began ministering as well. They sang *Withholding Nothing* by William McDowell, prompting the musicians to play just a little bit louder.

When Nicole finally settled down a little, Maiya spoke more words of comfort to her. "The Lord said, you are not what you did. You will no longer walk in shame. Embarrassment and guilt will not hold you hostage any longer." She dropped her head momentarily as those words that she just spoke into Nicole ripped through her like a double-edged sword. They instantly loosed Maiya from anything that may have been lingering from her past and was still attempting to hold her back.

Maiya lifted her head, half-speaking, half-crying in her prayer language. "Whew, Jesus!" she cried out, shaking her head, still alternating between her prayer language and English.

The quartet of anointed men nearest them also prayed in the Spirit, softly this time. Each had their eyes open, watching for additional opportunities to minister in this pivotal hour.

Maiya waved Van back over to bring her the microphone. When he brought it to her, he remained close.

"I've got to just tell y'all that God is restoring right now," Maiya said, looking up and around as she spoke. She remained on the floor with Nicole by the exit doors while she addressed the crowd.

The audience could still see her on the monitors although many of them were worshipping God with their hands lifted, heads bowed, and their eyes closed. Some of them looked up when they heard Maiya address them.

The worship team grew silent. The musicians returned to a softer tempo.

"You do not have to leave here the way you came. There is an anointing resting in this place for freedom and restoration." She took in a deep breath and then briefly shared some of her personal testimony.

"Let me tell you, the devil thought he had me, just like he thought he had you. But not today. Not anymore. We are free. We are restored. I almost didn't make it here. I almost didn't make it period. I was ready to kill myself. I was ready to kill somebody else. The pain was so great...but God," Maiya paused.

Angie walked over and handed Maiya a purple towel. She stayed close as well now.

"But God," Maiya reiterated, using the towel to wipe her face and then Nicole's too. "God did this!" She pointed to herself. "That's what God wants me to tell you. God healed me and He wants to heal you." She hugged Nicole even tighter. "He wants to restore you."

Nicole smiled as more tears stained her cheeks.

"It didn't happen all at once. It took time. It took prayer. It took love and me surrendering to Him. As a matter of fact, God just sealed my healing tonight. Beloved, will you surrender to God's healing tonight?" Maiya asked, stretching her left arm toward the crowd.

As Nicole's tears eventually subsided, Maiya motioned for Van to help them up. Bishop Horton assisted him, revealing a true servant's heart. Both men stayed close this time even after they were back upon their feet.

Maiya hugged Nicole again. "We're going to be fine. I love you." She motioned for Maria, who had also made her way closer to them, to escort Nicole back to her seat.

Maria nodded and led Nicole away.

"Thank You, Jesus!" Maiya exclaimed, slowly walking back to the front of the room with her remaining team members close behind. "This is what it's all about. We've got to pull somebody else out of the fire. Even someone we might have been estranged from."

Eyebrows suddenly lifted in the audience. Eyes looked intrigued.

Maiya took a deep breath and readied herself to address the curiosity that she sparked with her last statement.

CHAPTER TWENTY-EIGHT
Healed

"For those of you who are wondering, that precious woman I was travailing with on the floor is actually my birth mother," Maiya informed the audience. "I hugged her so much tonight, because I don't remember ever hugging her or her hugging me when I was around her. We've never had a healthy relationship, but God knows what He is doing and it's not about us, it's about Him."

People in the crowd nodded.

"The Lord wants me to share one more thing with you tonight and I'll be done," Maiya said as she wiped the remaining tears from her face and took a few more deep calming breaths.

The crowd waited with expectant looks. The musicians lifted the volume long enough for her to make it to the front before returning to a soft cadence as she prepared to speak again.

Maiya didn't immediately return to the stage. She stood still at the front, looking out at the crowd of people who remained standing. "I know this isn't probably how you all envisioned this night to be. It isn't how I envisioned it either, but His ways and thoughts are higher than ours. Everything that God does, in every way that He does it, is perfect and right, so I can't apologize for what God has done. But there is still some heaviness in this room. God sees you and He hears you." She literally saw spirits warring in the room.

Maiya paused to wipe her face again. She handed the towel to Angie, who was now standing next to her. "If you can and if you will, come down here with me. I want to pray with you." She beckoned the people to the altar with her right hand. "I've been where you are. My hurt may have been different from yours, but our God is the same. This same God can heal every hurt that you've ever experienced," she said, feeling a distinct peace from God that was familiar to her.

People almost ran to the front. They came from all over the building.

The rest of Maiya's team immediately got into place, standing on both sides of her. They were properly trained for this type of outpouring. Bishop Horton and the remaining ministers from the stage came down to assist as well.

"Don't worry about the voice that you hear, telling you that it can't happen for you," Maiya said, immediately addressing the spiritual tug-of-war that was still going on within so many of them. "God knows that it's been a struggle. He knows that some of you have truly been striving to live holy. He has seen you give everything you have to everybody only to get nothing in return. Your hurt is real and God is not overlooking your pain. Hear HIM in this place tonight," she pleaded.

"There are some other people that are so far out there in the world that you feel cut off," Maiya continued. "You are wondering if you'll ever experience what you had when you walked closely with the Lord. He sees you standing on the outside hoping to get back in. God sees you tonight. He wants you to come."

Women, men, and teenagers continued to make their way to the altar. Some came for salvation, others for restoration. Some came because they had tried everything else and finally decided to try Jesus.

"Don't worry about what's going to happen to the person who did what they did or said what they said to you. The Lord is saying vengeance is His. Forgive them. Forgive yourself. Your freedom and healing is in your forgiveness. It's time to let it go and move on," Maiya said, telling them some of the same things she told Nicole.

She made that plea to the immense crowd to release all their pent up burdens and lay aside the weights that held them down and kept them captive. She listened closely to the voice of the Lord, hearing what needed to be prayed over the people.

"The Lord said that tonight is the last night that you make Him your last option rather than your first choice. Somebody needs to make a solid choice for their lives before you leave here. In Jesus Name, I decree that every yoke of bondage is broken away from you now! Tonight is your night of restoration." Maiya spoke with great conviction and authority.

A robust mixture of sounds erupted in the building and spread like a wild fire. Shrill cries pierced the atmosphere. Wailing rose like an ocean wave, joined by high praise.

As they worshipped, Maiya bowed her head and pressed into prayer for healing and restoration for each person under the sound of her voice. "Beloved, I hear the Lord saying, healing is here." She lifted her head. "It's here now. The wait is over. Your restoration is here. Whatever has been troubling you, get ready for it to be your testimony. Whatever has plagued you, it's about to push you into your purpose. Those things that have beat you down are about to bless you. Whatever you lost, count it as gained. Whatever you sacrificed, count it restored. Everything that looked bad, the Lord said, look again. He's turning it around. It's working for your good!" she said, praying until the Spirit of the Lord released her.

When she ended the prayer, Maiya turned to walk up the stairs to the stage. "The Lord said, it's done," she continued, speaking much softer now. "As I prepare to leave, I want you to be empowered, encouraged, and strengthened to live in your healing from this day forward."

When Maiya reached the podium, she saw that Bishop Horton had followed her back to the stage as well. He stood off to the left with tears streaming down his face. She picked up her Bible and notebook from the podium, then walked over and handed the microphone to him.

"Thank you," Maiya said, embracing him briefly, yet fondly. Then instead of returning to her seat, she kept walking all the way backstage. Her team quickly followed.

"Lord, thank You!" Maiya said, walking with her head held high and her shoulders relaxed, yet evenly squared back. She was headed to live out God's declaration in her life – finally free and completely healed. She was living proof that His Word works.

"Well done, daughter," Bishop Horton said, smiling through his tears as he watched her walk away. "Well done." Then he turned to the crowd and dismissed the service with a short benediction.

Bishop Horton hadn't been the only one watching Maiya leave triumphantly. Napoleon had also watched her. He did so from his place near the back of the room, where he eased to after his failed attempt to distract her.

"Humph, I guess it's really over. What in the world was I thinking? I really need to get myself together," Napoleon said, looking at Maiya one last time before turning to face his own future without her. With his head bowed in defeat, he slowly walked toward the nearest exit and left.

* * * * *

LaJosie met Maiya in the hallway backstage. She held her stilettos, which had been given to her earlier by Angie. Saying nothing, she took Maiya's Bible and notebook and then handed over the shoes.

Maiya smiled and nodded her thanks. She carried her shoes as LaJosie led the way back to her dressing room. Her things had been packed up and were ready to go whenever she was.

That had been LaJosie's first completed assignment given by her new supervisor, Angie. She'd done it well.

When Maiya opened the door to the dressing room, Tony stepped from behind it, startling her and causing her to drop the shoes in her hands. She quickly recovered when she recognized who he was.

"What are you doing here?" Maiya asked, looking at him and then around the room slowly. Calla lilies of every color were placed everywhere.

"After a lengthy text conversation with Van earlier, he arranged for me to give you this pleasant surprise," Tony replied. "It *is* a pleasant surprise, isn't it?" He looked hopeful.

"Yes, I see that you remembered my favorite flower." Maiya smiled, returning her gaze to him just as her crew entered the room behind her. They all wore smiling faces, enjoying this little surprise just as much as she was.

"I remember everything about you, Maiya. I am your friend and always will be, but I love you and I'm in love with you," Tony said, suddenly turning serious. "I have stood by and watched you love other men. I've supported you every time, because I only wanted you to be happy. I just need one chance to prove my love to you. One chance to prove to you that *we* should be together." His eyes shimmered with tears.

Maiya was speechless.

When she didn't say anything after a few seconds, Tony continued, "I believe in you, I love the God in you and I want to try to do for you at least half of what you've done for so many others. May God have mercy on me if I give you anything less than my best." He held his right hand out to her. "I'm sent to restore, Maiya. One chance. That's all we need."

Still on mute, Maiya looked down at his hand, debating what she should do. For a brief moment, she felt that it was too soon to even consider another love and she didn't want to risk losing him as a friend. Just as quickly, she was reminded of the words she'd said earlier – God knows what He's doing. Restoration is not coming, it is here.

When she didn't answer, Tony looked just beyond her to Van, whom he knew she trusted beyond measure.

"Maiya." Van called her name gently.

She turned her head slightly, lifting her brows at him.

"Go!" her team yelled in unison.

Maiya smiled and put her forgotten shoes back on. She took Tony's waiting hand and followed him out of the room.

Angie slid her cell phone and purse into her free hand as she passed by.

Maiya smiled wider and shook her head at each one of them as she left the room. Loud cheers of happiness trailed them down the hallway as they exited the building...together.

The End

FINAL WORDS
From My Heart to Yours

From hurt to healing – it's the place that we often attempt to journey from. Many times we choose the wrong avenues, streets, and roads to travel. We make the One that should be our first and only option our very last. We try everything else before we reach for the Master's hand.

To those of you that have been hurt, wounded, trampled and tricked, I urge you to try Jesus! True healing can only come from the True Healer. The Bible declares in Isaiah 53:5 that He was wounded for our transgressions, bruised for our iniquities and the chastisement of our peace was upon Him and by His stripes we were healed. God wants you to know that it is already done. We must simply believe the Word of God, live according to that Word, and watch for the manifestation of that Word.

Now is not the time to sit back and wallow in your self-pity. It's your time to offer the sacrifice of praise. Give Him the praise that you really don't feel like giving, but you know without a doubt that God is surely worthy of. Offer God praise with the fruit of your lips, with the dance, with your talents, your time and your testimony.

Praise your way from hurt to healing. You don't have to stay trapped in the menace of your mind. The tape recorder doesn't have to continue to play over and over again. You have the authority to press STOP! The pain doesn't have to be the focus of every moment of every day.

The Bible declares that if we decree a thing, it shall be established in the earth for you. In Jesus Name, I decree that you are healed!

Broken hearts, be mended. Broken lives, be restored!

Broken relationships – be repaired and revived!

I declare that love will abide with you from this day forth. I pray that peace will reign in every area of your life.

God's Word says, give and it shall be given unto you, pressed down, shaken together and running over shall I cause men to give unto your bosom.

Many people say, name it and claim it. Jesus said, only believe!

Believe God for all that you need today. Delight yourself in the Lord and believe Him that you will receive the desires of your heart. Stand in the presence of the Most High God. Bask in the glow of His love. Lift your hands and bless the Lord Jesus!

We can't stop pressing into Him! Press on in your praise! Press on in your prayer life! Press on in your study time! Press on in your service!

The Bible teaches us that as we draw nigh unto God, He will draw nigh unto us. God is near to those who are brokenhearted and with a contrite spirit. He is waiting for you! Healing is waiting for you! This is the Word of the Lord concerning your life!

Hurt to Healing isn't just a book, it's a journey! Today is your day. This is your moment!

Finally, while I hope that you have enjoyed the story part of this book, my prayer is that you have not missed the message. Whatever you are seeking – it is in Christ Jesus. Beloved, now is a great time to begin your journey from hurt to your *own* promised healing!

~ Prophetess LaTrice Williams

ABOUT THE AUTHOR

LaTrice Williams is God's servant, first and foremost. She is mother to many beautiful children, two of which she had biologically. She is the CEO and founder of *LaTrice Williams Ministries* and *The Living With More* Brand. She is the editor-in-chief of the *Living With More* national newsletter. In addition to *Hurt to Healing*, she is also the author of *Life's Experience*.

As an ordained minister of the Gospel, LaTrice enjoys sharing the Word of God through many avenues. She will literally preach and teach her shoes off as she endeavors to empower, encourage and strengthen others to pursue their passion, live in wholeness and receive the healing that is available for their lives.

www.ingramcontent.com/pod-product-compliance
Lightning Source LLC
Chambersburg PA
CBHW070039260626
47159CB00005B/2080